2.99

Copyright © 2007 by Leia Tiedeman. All rights reserved.
Cover Art by Anna Allen, Copyright © 2007 by Leia Tiedeman
Mica Moon characters, names and related items are trademarks owned by Leia Tiedeman.

No part of this publication may be reproduced. Stored in a retrieval system, or transmitted in any form or by any means, electronic, mechanical, photocopying, recording, or otherwise, without written permission of the author.

This is a work of fiction. Names, characters, places, and incidents either are the product of the authors imagination or are used fictitiously. Any resemblance to actual persons, live or dead are purely coincidental.

For information on reproducing sections of this book, or sales of this book go to www.micamoonbooks.com
micamoonbooks@gmail.com

Published by
Indigo House Publishing
IndigoHousePublishing@gmail.com

ISBN: 978-0-615-17978-0

Printed in the United States of America

This book is available in discounts for schools, please call 480-703-9537

Leia Stone
Scottsdale, AZ 85254
micamoonbooks@gmail.com
www.MicaMoonBooks.com

I must say that if you have stumbled across this book, you are very special. I would like to introduce you to the first installment of my young adult, fantasy-fiction series novel entitled *Mica Moon and The Domed Cities*. If you find any editing mistakes, please forgive me. Unfortunately, I am human. Thank you for supporting Mica Moon, and her message to the world. Stay tuned for the next Mica Moon book, entitled *Mica Moon and The Crystal Skulls*.

Namaste,
Leia Stone

To my four soul mates:

Mimi, my grandmother in spirit, for her inspiration and divine guidance. **Chad**, my brother, for always pushing me to succeed. **Buddha**, my dog, for showing me how to love unconditionally. And to **Cynthia**, my mother, for teaching me I can do anything, even change the world. Without you, I am misplaced. I love you all endlessly…

Contents

One

· The Crystal Healer · 1

Two

· The World Leader · 21

Three

· Dylan Pierce · 38

Four

· The Gypsies · 55

Five

· Harvard · 77

Six

· New World · 94

Seven

· Lady Evil · 112

Eight

· Ronak · 130

Nine

· The Universal School of Lightworkers · 150

Ten

· The Akashic Records · 169

Eleven

· The Domed World · 186

Twelve

· The Hanging · 204

With love and light, I introduce *Mica Moon and The Domed Cities*.

Mica Moon and The Domed Cities

Book 1

To contact the author call (480)-703-9537

or email: MicaMoonBooks@gmail.com

Author: Leia Stone

Cover Art: Anna Allen

www.MicaMoonBooks.com

Chapter One
The Crystal Healer

Every morning she looked out that window hoping to see a different reality and this day was no different. Mica, wickedly tired, sat up slowly this morning, faced her window and opened her eyelids. The artificial sun shone on her bright blonde hair, so pale it was almost white, her fair skin glowed, and her baby blue eyes squinted. She walked over to the window and sighed.

Only fourteen years of age and already she felt like an old woman. What she saw this morning was the same as every other, a huge piece of plastic cut right into the backyard, drawing the perimeter of captivity. She had always lived in the domed world, but felt like she knew what it had once been like as a human in the free world. She stared at the big man-made robotic bubble cutting into the very core of mother Earth and sighed again.

The domes, like upside down salad bowls containing life, covered every major city in every country; they were their only hope. The domes were made of millions of tiny microscopic Nano-robots that could regenerate, self-replicate and grow. They always knew when to purify and recycle the air, when to rain, and when to block out the deadly sunlight. They were rigged with safety alarms that sounded if any sick air from the outside leaked in, but lately the alarms were going off all to often. Worst of all, the domes were programmed to lock out the ID positive contaminated humans and lock in the clean ones. It was as though the domes were alive. As if they were a robotic ozone layer.

Outside, beyond the domes, was a deadly place to inhabit. It was so dark with pollution Mica could barely make out the little hand pressed against the translucent wall that confined the city and kept them safe from the sick air and soil. When she recognized the little human child's hand for what it was, her heart stopped. She took a deep breath and her spirit wept as she looked at that hand, then she let out a groan that woke her dog Buddha, who leapt off the bed.

Mica grabbed her purple velvet purse, and Buddha followed her out the bedroom door. Tears were streaming down Mica's face as she crossed the backyard and sat right in front of injustice and cruelty. Buddha sat next to her wagging his tail in anxiety. She stood divided, every cell in her body rebelled against the truth. She was safe on the inside and this poor soul was out there baking in the deadly sun and drinking the blackened water, contaminated with the virus.

The plan to dome the cities started when global warming began to threaten human survival but the virus was what rushed the government into action. A virus that spread like the flu began to engulf human bodies, killing as severely as AIDS, but faster. The domes quickly became a quarantine, so that not only were the contaminated ones living outside, sick with disease but they also battled pollution, heat, floods and famine. The sun was so intense in some areas that even through the dark polluted air it damaged anything in its path heating the Earth like an oven close to 130 degrees.

Mica wanted to split open these walls of confinement and let every living thing on the outside reap the benefits of a safe world but she knew she was no better off inside these structures in the long run. The Nanobots were sick too and couldn't hold the domed environment together much longer. People inside the domes were getting contaminated through leaks and being ejected outside to fight for their lives. The scientists couldn't figure out why the Nanobots had begun to fail. So in the end maybe Mica would be the one infected, be the one drinking the blackened water and breathing the sick air.

She reached for the hand and put hers over it, between them it was almost as though the Nanobots could feel the pain and desperation, and wanted to disappear and end this misery. The clear plastic wall was over ten inches thick, but she swore she could feel heat from the life of the body on the other side. In some parts it was only five inches thick. The domes were thinning and dying, and Mica was the only one who would admit it.

"What has become of the world?" she breathed.

The hand quivered in excitement and desperation, the air on the other side was so dark, Mica could barely see the outline of his body. He moved closer showing a dirty, sunken in, ill face of a broken child. The boy moved his lips slowly, like it was the most important thing he would ever say, "There are hundreds of people out here, men, woman and children. Please help, we're sick, they have stopped sending us medicines and water... open the dome, we can't breathe, no food, can't...live... like this." Mica couldn't hear his voice but caught every word reading his lips; she didn't even blink for she knew she was his only hope.

She just couldn't comprehend the fact that she really lived in a world where people had to be purposefully tortured with no relief or aid. Mica stared into his deep brown eyes and saw so much pain, she saw injustice and she felt sick. She spoke back with fragile composure, delivering a death sentence.

"The domed world is sealed to the contaminated forever. There are no entries for you. I can't help, I'm sorry. This isn't fair."

The little boy's eyes widened and he pulled his face back and put his hand on the plastic wall, his fingers were scarred and deformed and his palm was caked in dirt. Mica reached into her purple bag and pulled out three shiny orange crystals and laid them on her lap, and then she put her hand over his and felt so much love, gratitude and sorrow for this young brave child.

Tears streamed from her face, and after a few moments Mica started seeing the familiar golden light flood out of her palm through the plastic and illuminate the boy on the other side, his body was bathed in a golden glow and his beautiful face was widened in shock. Mica closed her eyes, placed both hands on the dome, and released as much healing energy as she could bear into the little boy on the outside. She figured it was the least she could do. After a few minutes she opened her eyes, and when there was no more light left she removed her hand from the dome. The little boy clawed at the plastic, wondering where Mica had gone, his hands no longer scarred but she had no more energy left for him, he had gotten all he was meant to. She was hungry and needed to eat and she knew there was nothing more she could do for this little boy today.

"Come back tomorrow, bring your friends. I'll do what I can," she mouthed.

She picked up her bag and left the crystals in front of the dome and walked away, knowing he didn't want her to leave, knowing it was a cold thing to do, and headed towards the house.

Once inside, she crossed the living room into the kitchen, the TV was on loud, and she heard the newswoman speaking while she poured her cereal and soy milk.

"It's been forty years today since the domes were created with Nano technology in 2012 in a heroic attempt to save humanity. There have still been many sightings of life on the outside, but today I think I speak for everyone when I say it's good to be in here! The United Nations continues to bring food, water and medicine to the contaminated outside but say that their stockpiles are dwindling.

Recent scares have been reported about the Nanobots depleting and rumors have begun that the domes are going to disappear and that we will all persish. We want to clarify that we all knew the domes were a temporary solution to keeping us safe from the deadly world outside, and all attempts are being made to reinforce the technology created to make the domes continue forever. Scientists are working on a bigger, better, longer-lasting dome model, so have no worries.

"I'm Susan Bleeker reporting from Sedona, Arizona and with only a population of 2,000 people, we are fortunate to even have become a domed city. We are lucky that World Leader Mullen's father, Hugh Mullen, saw Sedona as a beautiful treasure that should be preserved. As you all know, after the outbreak of the ID virus, and the global warming travesties the heads of all of the countries got together and called for peace in a united attempt to save the human race, electing one World Leader. Cities of one million or more were domed and no more than three domes per state, because of the cost of Nano technology and the time factor. All of the clean humans were given a place to stay inside the domes and the contaminated were kept outside for our protection. Doctors are still working on a cure for the virus so that our contaminated loved ones may one day be able to return home, if they're still alive by then. Death rates on the outside are dangerously high.

"We have Hugh Mullen Jr. to thank for doming Phoenix, Tucson, and Sedona. It was devastating to those contaminated with the ID virus and our hearts go out to those who were locked out, but we made history here on Earth by erecting thousands of domes in just three months!

"Every man, woman, and child worked either in the factories or in the assembly line and what we have today is a beautiful preservation of our lives. So on this forty year anniversary we would like to thank everyone for contributing, especially World Leader Mullen who was elected in 2013 to be the first World Leader at only age twenty five. We count on him to converse with each country leader and to make fair and just decisions for the conservation of the world." The woman looked to her partner who was dressed in a blue suit and wore a plastic smile.

Mica rolled her eyes at this woman's enthusiasm. She thought of all the people who hadn't made it to the major cities that were being domed and were locked out and infected by the virus. She thought of the little boy outside and wondered how many more people were out there and how much longer they could survive. Mica got up to leave when the woman on the news stood erect and started speaking loudly.

"What's this? Breaking news! World Leader Mullen has fallen ill, he's at state hospital in Washington D.C, in critical condition. That's all we know, but we will get more news for you on that later. Meanwhile, American dome leader Damian Black will be filling in for the World Leader until Mullen is on his feet again."

Mica's ears perked up at that. She sat back down facing the TV catching a glimpse of the sweet old man's face.

Mica liked World Leader Mullen; she even met him once when he came to Sedona to speak last year on peace in the domes. He walked right up to her after the speech and shook her hand, he said he had heard of the famous crystal healer from Sedona but did not know she was just a little girl, Mica had puffed up her chest at that and boasted that she was almost fourteen years old. He had laughed and said he hoped to see her again. She didn't see any sickness on his body then and wondered what was wrong.

She felt sad that he was ill and wondered what the world would do if he died. World Leader Mullen's father, Hugh, was one of the original dome engineers, and he'd helped save all the people right after they started getting sick and people's homes started getting eaten up by the ocean. It was rumored that without the solution of the domes the government was going to begin mass discarding of contaminated ones, killing them all in an effort to save the clean ones. When Hugh and his son stepped in with the Nanobot technology, they saved millions of humans. They really fought for erecting a dome over Sedona. It was such a small town most people said it wasn't worth it, but Hugh knew it was a special place and insisted. Mica heard creaking on the stairs and saw Gran making her way down to the kitchen.

"Gran, World Leader Mullen is sick and in the hospital!" Mica shrieked desperately.

"Well, good morning to you, too," Gran said.

"Oh, sorry, good morning Gran," Mica said smiling.

Gran had her silver hair tied in the usual tight bun and wore a pink nightgown, her brown eyes squinted beneath her wrinkles.

"I heard the World Leader fell ill upstairs on my bedroom TV. It's a sad day for the world, child. He really wanted a better place for us, but everyone has their day as you know."

"Yeah, I know." Mica looked down at her feet, thinking about death. She decided to change the subject.

"Is it true the domes are going to disappear?" Mica asked.

"Well, I hope not but Nano technology was an experiment in those days, honey, little robots that think for themselves. It's still a scary thought. I don't imagine they can stand up to the harsh conditions much longer, everything has its time to break down, even machines. The Nanobots are like billions of little computers and can get viruses and get sick, and if one gets sick, they all get sick, because they're connected."

"So, they're sick?" Mica asked, wondering how Gran knew so much about the world.

"Yes, they're sick. Were you outside this morning? I heard the door earlier?"

"Oh yeah! I saw another person locked out today; I wish they could just dig under the dome or break in or something. It's not fair!"

"Oh, bite your tongue! You know good and well that would be bad for us all and that the Nanobots are programmed to resist that sort of thing. If an infected one gets near one of the exits, the lasers on the domes scan the iris of their eyes and can tell if that person has the ID virus. It is for our own safety, honey."

Mica looked down at the ground. "I know, but it's not fair."

"Oh, you're such a bleeding heart, always feeling the pain of the world's suffering. Smile, dear child and don't forget to rinse your bowl." Mica rinsed her bowl of cereal thinking of the Nano-bots. Were they conscious? Would they stop filtering the air and become rogue and spew in dark, disease-infested winds to show people on the inside, what it was like outside? If they disappeared, then everyone would get sick and eventually die. Mica shook off the thought.

"Gran, can we go to the crystal shop? I need some more crystals for Mrs. Walsh's healing today."

"Of course. So, Mrs. Walsh made an appointment, did she? Have her kidneys been acting crazy again? You know I think it's all that drinking she does down at the tavern, but I'm not one to gossip. You just let me know if you see anything else wrong with her so I can put her in my nightly prayers," Gran said.

Gran loved to gossip, and Mica knew she would pray for Mrs. Walsh but she would also tell half the town anything Mica told her about their healing session.

"OK, come get me when you're ready. I'll be up in my room, come on Boo." Mica trotted upstairs with Buddha.

As she stared out the window once more, Mica quoted an old tourism book in her head.

"Sedona is a vast land, full of deep red rock, crisp cold creeks and orange cranberry sunsets." Mica read old books dating back to the year 2000 and the pictures they showed of old Sedona were nothing like its current state. Although the mountains were still breathtaking, the plant life was wilting and Mica had never seen a cranberry sunset, although she longed too. The Nanobots shone artificial filtered U/V rays through every dome but nothing close to a cranberry sunset.

Mica felt a pang of sadness as she thought of her life in this small place. For some reason she felt as if she would never see Sedona again. The world had a way of doing that. Living in these domed cities made you feel all hope was gone for a normal life. You felt trapped, crammed into this living space with plastic fifty feet over your head to call your shelter. Mica longed to see the ocean, the sky, to feel the natural rain on her face, all of the things she'd read in books about how life used to be. Now it only rained when the engineers wanted it to, and they warned you before hand, so it took all of the fun out of it.

She turned from the window and started looking through her giant cabinet of gemstones and made a list of the ones she needed for Mrs. Walsh's healing. Mica was really proud of her collection and felt lucky to have crystals from all over the world. Last year the local news did a ten-minute piece on Mica and her ability to heal diseases with rocks and crystals. After that, people sent her precious stones from all over the world. The government wouldn't allow Mica to go outside to try and heal the contaminated ones. They said it was too dangerous and if she got the virus she wouldn't be able to heal people anymore. They had told her that they needed her safe and alive. She hoped after a few more times working with the little boy she could heal him.

She grabbed a few dark blue lapis lazuli stones from Brazil. She put one in her pocket and slid the other one around the metal ring on Buddha's collar for energy protection, since they were going into town and lots of people would be there.

People here in Sedona liked Mica and most revered her as the crystal healer, even doctors sent her patients they could not cure. People took trains through the traveling tunnels for weeks just for Mica to heal them. Some people came from far parts of the world like China to be healed but a few thought she was a witch and meant her harm. Mica felt sorry for those people and forgave them for not knowing the truth. The truth is, Mica was just different, not a witch, not a demon. She was just a girl who believed in the healing ability of herself and her magical rocks and saw what no one else could see, but was definitely there, an aura.

Everyone Mica had ever met had a big, bright aura, the energy field surrounding the body. When she was little she didn't understand why other children couldn't see it. The colors around people's heads and the glowing light coming off their bodies was right there, yet no one else saw it. When kids started making fun of her, she stopped talking about it.

Most times, when people came to Mica they would ask at the end of their session, "Will I be all right?" In the beginning of her days as a healer, Mica used to tell people the truth, that she didn't know, but after a while she started telling everyone, "Yes, you will be fine." She wasn't a psychic and never claimed to be, but for some reason people thought since she could tell what was wrong with them and heal them, that she could also tell the future. Mica found that if she told everyone they would be fine, most of the people were, and never had to see her again. The power of positive thinking really worked and Mica did it often; she was a dreamer. But there were some people so weak with barely any life force left that Mica told them they might die so they could prepare.

She was seven years old when she found Buddha and did her first healing. He was behind one of the shops in town; he had no collar and his thin, malnourished body convulsed wildly. He was wet all over and so sick he barely had any aura left, just a few golden glimmers. That's when Mica found out she could not only see these people's life force energy and know when they were low and sick, but that she could also heal them. She could make them stronger and brighter by giving them some of her energy that never seemed to deplete. Gran was there that day behind the shop and ever since then she encouraged Mica to believe in herself and be a healer.

That day when Mica found Buddha, she wept over him and grabbed him in her arms, and when she held him close to her heart, she saw her blue sparkly aura shooting golden and white shafts of light into Buddha's body and he began to twitch and gain strength.

His inner light began to grow bigger and brighter. From then on she knew when people were sick and how she could heal them. Everyone seemed to have this energy in him or her, this life force, or this aura. The sick old people dying in hospitals have a faint glow about them with dark muddy colors, while young, lively children had a light glowing at least a foot off their bodies in bright, vibrant colors. Once Mica realized she could help expand and grow this life force, she set out to heal people. She found that certain gemstones and rocks contained different energies and she could put her energy in them and give them to a sick person to carry around like medicine. Mica began laying the stones on the low energy spots of a sick person during their healings and that's how she became "Mica the crystal healer" in her town. A loud knock at the door jerked her back to reality.

"Ready to go dear?" Gran yelled.

"Meet you downstairs," Mica called back.

She grabbed her purple velvet bag and some money out of her donations jar that she'd collected from her healings and closed the large oak cabinet. Buddha trailed after her, wagging his tail. He knew they were going to town and he loved the attention he got from people for being so cute. His fluffy brown hair danced as he walked. He had a flat nose and bulging eyes but somehow still managed to look overly adorable.

"You can't go today Buddha, you have to stay here." Mica looked back and teased him.

Buddha halted, and shaking his rear vigorously, he let out a little whimper.

Mica laughed. "Oh, come on, you know I wouldn't leave you!"

He leapt into her arms and licked her face. She giggled and smoothed his hair before sticking him in her velvet bag, his head peeking out. He was a tiny dog, a runt, weighing only about six pounds but he had the spirit of a lion. When she got to the kitchen, Gran had her purse over her shoulder and house keys out.

Mica stopped dead in her tracks and stared at Gran's heart. Mica was used to turning off her ability to see peoples auras and sicknesses during mundane daily tasks. Then, when she wanted to she just concentrated and would see a person's energy field easily. But sometimes when she wasn't paying attention and someone was really sick she just saw their aura even though she didn't turn it on, as if that person was crying out for help. Right now she saw that Gran had a black cloud over her heart and Mica felt sick at the thought of what it could mean. Gran's normally reddish and yellow aura looked sick.

"What are you staring at dear? You look like you've seen a ghost." Gran's face was contorted, as if trying to figure out what had shocked Mica.

"Something's wrong with you," was all Mica could say.

Gran touched her heart as if she already knew what Mica had seen and said, "I'm fine," and walked out the door to their bikes.

Mica pulled her bike up to the crystal shop and realized she and Gran hadn't spoken a word the whole ride. She walked through the crystal shop doors with Gran. Buddha was nestled in her bag. As they were looking around the store, they realized almost everything was gone, every good crystal had been sold. The owner of the shop, Tad Nickels, said that two men in black suits carrying a big steel case had come in and bought almost every gem he had. Tad seemed happy but also curious.

"They made me a lot of money today, but when I asked them what they needed all them crystals for, they smiled and left. Said nothin," Tad said with a southern accent.

So Mica just picked out a few amethysts and bloodstones she needed for today, and Gran walked outside while Mica paid.

"Mica, you're the only one around here who would have a need for all those crystals. What do you reckon they're up to?" Tad inquired.

"Well, I dunno, maybe I've got some competition," Mica said jokingly, smiling. The truth is a lot of people collected crystals for their beauty, but Tad seemed to like getting into people's personal affairs. Mica finished paying for the crystals and walked outside. As soon as Mica stepped out the door she saw that Gran was on her cell phone.

"The time has come? Right now? Oh, I've got to go," said Gran as she sensed Mica was behind her. Gran snapped the phone shut and whipped around with a big smile.

"Did you get everything you needed?" Gran said.

"Who was that, Gran?"

"Don't worry about it, darling. Let's get home." Gran's face was drained of color and she looked sad, Mica thought.

Buddha peeked out of his hiding place, and Mica set him on the ground. They headed home in silence. Mica was biking behind Gran when she noticed that the black spot around her heart was getting bigger by the second. Mica let a tear fall off her cheek. She debated in her mind whether or not Gran was going to have a heart attack and what she would do without her. Mica had been only a week old when Gran adopted her. Even though she wasn't her real grandma, Mica called her Gran and felt she was the only person in the world who truly knew her. She had always felt so loved and accepted by Gran.

As they arrived at home, a big white SUV was parked in the driveway. Not many people owned cars anymore, because they were bad for the environment; only the government and rich people could afford to have them converted to run on water or electric, not gas.

Before Mica could even ask whose car it was, Gran turned to her and tears were streaming down her face, the blackness around her chest was so big now you could barely make out her face through the dark aura.

"Oh, Gran, what's wrong?"

* Mica Moon And The Domed Cities *

Mica walked up and laid her hands on her beloved Gran's heart and took a deep breath. When she exhaled she released a vast amount of golden healing energy into Gran's chest, but once it hit her heart it bounced off and came right back at Mica. Mica widened her eyes in bewilderment. She couldn't heal her.

"You can't help me child," Gran said as she pulled Mica's hands down and held them.

Gran spoke, "Dear, we only have a few minutes to talk. I'm not going to die, my heart isn't sick, it's just broken. I'm sad, OK?"

"What are you sad about?"

"Sweetie," Gran said, "you know that your parents died and shortly after you were adopted by me, right?"

"Yeah," Mica said, tears welling up her eyes.

"Well, the truth is they were murdered, and your real birth grandfather called and he's sick and needs to talk to you. We are old friends and after your parents died he gave you to me to adopt you for safekeeping. His daughter was your mother. His wife, your grandmother had died of cancer many years ago and I was the only one left in the world he could trust."

"Huh?" Mica's head swam with confusion and shock. "You know my real grandpa? Keep me safe from whom? You knew my parents?"

"Yes, I did, I was your mother's nanny when she was young and your grandfather is your only living relative. Honey, there's no real time to explain, your grandpa will explain it all to you, but you must hurry."

"What's going on? I don't understand."

"My heart is broken because I knew I was losing you today; I love you very much, but you must go meet your grandfather today and you won't be back here to see me for a very long time."

Mica sobbed. "I don't want to go. I don't want to leave you. Why can't he come here? I can't do this, I'm too young to go alone. I won't leave Buddha either, he's mine forever!" Mica shouted.

"You can take Buddha. Now let's go inside, we haven't a minute to waste."

They walked inside and standing right there in the kitchen were the two men in black suits, carrying a silver case from the crystal shop. One of the men in the black suit stood up, grabbed the silver case and said, "Ms. Mica Foster, you have three minutes to pack your personal things and come with us to heal the World Leader. This steel case has every crystal you will ever need. Go now. Two minutes or we will miss our jet."

Mica stood there for 30 seconds with her mouth open. World Leader Mullen was her grandfather? She was going on a jet? Two minutes!!! Ahhhhh! Mica thought.

Gran gently nudged the small of her back and led her upstairs to her bedroom. Buddha followed looking confused. Gran took out a large tan duffle bag, and she and Mica started shoving anything they could into it.

"World Leader Mullen is my grandpa?" Mica asked, putting the pieces of the puzzle together in her mind.

"Yes, Mica, and he loves you very much, he will explain everything. I have prepared for this day since I got you. You are a very special girl, but you can't stay here healing the town's people forever. You have greater tasks my dear." She zipped up Mica's bag and started to head down the stairs.

"Wait, Gran! There's a boy locked outside the domes and he thinks I'm meeting him tomorrow in the backyard. Will you go to him in the morning and tell him I had to go but everything's going to be alright, that I'll figure something out."

"Okay, dear, you have my word, I will."

At the end of the stairs the men grabbed the bag from Gran. She turned to Mica and gave her a big hug. Then she whispered in her ear, "No one else knows World Leader Mullen is your grandfather. Don't tell anyone, it's for your protection. He has requested your presence as his healer, not his family. Good luck and I love you more than all the stars in the sky and I'll always be here for you."

"I love you too and I'm scared," was all Mica could say.

Mica picked up Buddha and followed the two men into the white SUV and set off to heal the World Leader … her grandfather.

Chapter Two
The World Leader

On the way to the small Sedona airport, the two men didn't say a word and Mica was glad. She needed to be alone with her thoughts; she sat with Buddha on her lap looking out the window. The trees that once hung lusciously over the highway were now brown and sickly. Mica remembered being younger when the trees were green and full. Now it seemed the soil was rejecting everything that tried to live.

The food inside the domes was bland tasting and genetically engineered, but Gran had told Mica stories of what rich foods tasted like before the domes. She'd told Mica of berries that grew in the wild and not in a science lab. Global warming had caused the seas to rise and a fungus began to grow in the soil, killing all the crops. Everyone was so paranoid about contracting the ID virus, that everything that could be sterilely lab engineered was.

The SUV turned the corner and pulled up to a private jet-way. The two men were whispering and talking into the sleeves of their shirts. Mica got a bad feeling and Buddha began to whine restlessly.

"Is everything OK?" squeaked Mica in a nervous voice.

"We're fine," said one of the men.

They pulled the white SUV right up to the door of the jet. Then they both pulled out guns and said, "stay down," and opened the door.

Stay down!!! You just said everything was OK!!! Mica was screaming inside her head. Guns were outlawed forty years ago, even for government officials, it was part of the dome peace treaty. Why did they need guns? Just as she thought it, she got her answer. Shots fired all around her and Mica grabbed Buddha and crawled under the big back seat and put her duffle bag over them. One of the windows blew out and glass sprinkled on the duffle bag and stuck in Mica's long platinum blonde hair. The noise sounded like fireworks right inside the car. Was she going to die before she even got to meet her grandpa or kiss a boy for the first time? She was only fourteen!

The shooting stopped and the back door opened. It was one of the men who drove her here, his shoulder was bleeding.

"Get out. Run to the jet. It's safe for now." And then he collapsed.

Mica jumped up, grabbed her duffle bag and the silver case. Buddha ran behind her with his head hung low. She struggled to get all of the bags up the steps to the jet with her purple purse slung over her shoulder. She got to the door, and the Captain appeared, pulling her and Buddha into the plane. She turned around and saw five men dead on the ground and the one man who was shot in the shoulder moaning.

"Wait!" Mica said.

"I'm not leaving without him," and she pointed to the man.

The captain whispered a curse word under his breath and ran out of the plane, dragging in the bleeding man. Then he slammed the door shut and his co-pilot started them down the runway. Mica looked through the window and saw a few dark figures running towards the plane, shooting at it. The tips of their guns were flickering with light but the plane was in the air a bit now and was not damaged by the bullets.

Mica was in shock. She had never seen a gun, much less been fired at, she wanted answers as to WHY the people were shooting, but right now she needed to help the man who had helped her and been shot for it. She grabbed a clear quartz crystal, a sunstone, and an amethyst shard and walked over to the man. Buddha jumped up into one of the seats and rested his head on his paws watching.

"I can help you," Mica said.

"OK," said the man weakly, knowing her reputation. He reclined in his seat feeling faint.

Mica began laying the stones on his neck and stomach, and then she took her hands and gently laid them on his blood-soaked shoulder. She took a deep breath and focused on his aura and saw that his life force energy was weak but okay. There was a large muddy black gap in his aura around his shoulder, and the energy was pulling away with each drop of blood he lost. It was low, but not the worst she had ever seen. She willed his blood to flow away from the hole in the shoulder. In her head she told every cell of his body that the hole wasn't there, trying to misguide their memory of the gaping wound. The golden light flew out of her hands and covered his entire body like a cocoon. She sat there for a long time giving him everything she had. She knew she should keep some for herself, but she also knew that he needed everything she could give. She gave and gave for three hours and then she collapsed into a deep sleep.

The man opened his eyes and moved his arm in wonderment. The hole was still there and would need stitches but he had no pain, and the bleeding had stopped and a scab had begun to cover the hole! He had heard of this little girl and her healings, but had no idea what she was capable of. He picked up Mica and laid her lengthwise across three seats. He kissed her cheek in gratitude, and then went back to his seat and went to sleep himself.

A while later, the pilot shook them both awake.

"How long did I sleep?" Mica asked in a low dazed voice.

"About six hours," said the pilot.

"Six hours!!!" said Mica and the man in unison.

"Well where are we? Surely we should be in Washington by now!" Mica asked perplexed.

"We should be in India in about three hours, Miss Mica."

"India!" Mica remarked, "I thought the World Leader was in Washington? AND what were those men shooting at?"

The pilot was silent. Mica glared at him, ever since she found out she was the World Leader's granddaughter she felt a bit like royalty, and so she stood up and said, "I demand an answer, what were the men shooting at?" The tone of sassiness in her voice made Buddha stand up as well and give a low growl.

"They were shooting at you, Miss Foster, here eat something, you must be hungry," He handed her and the injured man sandwiches and soymilk and walked away.

"Me?" Mica said breathlessly. Did those people know she was the World Leader 's granddaughter? But if they did why would that anger them? She decided to just wait and ask her grandfather himself.

"Thank you for saving my life, Mica. My name is Dominic, but my friends call me Dom," said the injured man. "You know for a second there, I thought I was dead and you were an angel or a character from a fairytale, with your long white hair."

"You're welcome. Thank you for getting me on the plane, I feel like I'm in a dream, maybe this is a fairytale. Is this a dream?" Mica wondered aloud.

"No this is very real," said Dom, "So how do you, I mean, what it is that… well, I can't believe you really healed me with your hands and those rocks, I mean they're just rocks, right?" Dom said.

"To you they are but to me they are vessels of healing light and energy."

"Oh," Dom replied arching his eyebrows.

"Dom? How are we flying outside the domes? Are there giant long straw-like tunnels in the sky connecting the domes like there are for the trains on the ground?"

Dom smiled, "No. Unlike the ground traveling tunnels, which are like giant straws, sky travel is different. The Nanobots thin a certain area of the dome and create a suction projecting the plane out of the dome while not letting any sick air in. Then the plane is specially engineered to resist the heat of the sun and pollution. The pilots fly guided by computers."

"Oh, how do you know all of this?" Mica wondered.

"I work for the government." Dom smiled.

"Do you remember the world before the domes?" Mica asked him.

She knew he would be fine until they could get him to a hospital, but he was still weak and it showed in his strained voice.

"No, I wasn't born yet. I'm thirty-six, but my parents told me many stories about the way it used to be. People would just throw trash on the ground and it would go to big empty lands and then they would burn it out in the open."

Mica gasped at that.

"I know!" Dom said, "In the domes we realize how precious clean air is, but before the domes, the people didn't realize the ozone layer was their dome. They thought they didn't have a dome and they could do what they wanted to the air, and it would just evaporate."

"Well, it didn't, and now we have to pay for it!" Mica said with fury.

"I know, my uncle lived in a small town in New Mexico. He was camping for three weeks, my mom had no way of getting a hold of him and...he was locked out. Then he got contaminated. We haven't heard from him since."

Mica scanned his aura and saw a small black pea-sized blob flutter briefly over his heart as he spoke about his uncle. This was Mica's way of knowing whether or not she could trust that people were telling the truth. When they spoke of sad things, it would be reflected in their auras, or if they lied their aura would contain red, agitated, nervous energy. Dom's was soothing, sad, and green with dark blue.

"I'm sorry about your uncle, Dom. I'm going to figure out a way to make the Earth and the infected better again. I'll go to college and I'll study science and I'll invent something. I'll figure something out, I've got to." Mica said this matter-of-factly.

"I think you can do whatever you want in life, you're very special. Don't ever let anyone tell you that you can't change the world." He said. Mica smiled and laid her head on the seat, petting Buddha.

Once the plane landed, Dom went right to the emergency room, and Mica went with a man to see the World Leader. Every time one of the men said the "World Leader," Mica would say, "my grandpa" in her head. What was she supposed to do when she saw him? Did he expect a hug or just for her to heal him and leave? After she healed him would he take her to dinner so they could talk, or did he just want to get better and get back to work?

The drive to where he was staying fascinated Mica. She loved India. The dirt roads, the food carts, the dark-skinned children running around in bright silk wraps, the praying in public, the beaded fabric, the colors, the smells. She felt like she had been here before as if she was finally home. Mica loved India the moment she stepped foot on its warm brown soil.

They arrived at a large iron gate and a man with a shaved head and orange silk-wrap came and opened it.

"Why does that man look like that?" Mica asked her driver.

"Because he's a monk and this is a sacred monastery."

A monastery! Cool! Mica thought. She figured her grandpa would be at the hospital, so he must not even be that sick. She'd seen a movie once about monks and she was excited to see one up close. They drove along the curved road for a while before a stone castle appeared. It was amazing. It had big pillars and large domes made of gold at the top of the large structure.

The driver parked the car, got out and opened the door for Mica and Buddha. A monk came over and spoke into the driver's ear and the driver said, "No, I'm not leaving. She needs protection." The monk leaned closer and spoke a little longer this time. The driver threw Mica's bag on the ground and took out her steel crystal travel box and then got in the car and drove off. The monk turned to Mica and gave her a hug, picking her up and spinning her around. Mica giggled wildly. Then he set her down.

"I've been waiting a LONG time to meet you, angel, let's get you right in to see your grandfather," the monk said.

"You know he's my grandpa?" Mica said in astonishment.

The monk's aura consisted purely of white, something she had never seen before.

"Yes, I know, we are close friends. He trusts me. Besides a monk can't break a promise to another, bad karma and all of that." The monk smiled, teasing her.

He brought her and Buddha to a pair of large oversized wooden doors. The doors stood twenty feet tall and one rested slightly open. Then he bowed to her and walked away. She stood there, not knowing what to do. Mica continued to stand there for moment, until Buddha barked loudly.

"Mica you can come in," came a voice from the room.

She timidly pushed open the door and a tear fell from her face. It was him, World Leader Mullen, her grandpa and he was deathly sick. He was so pale and dry looking, as if he was shriveling up. He barely had any life force left; his aura was dark and very small.

"Come here, child," he said pointing to a chair beside his bed.

"Hi," was all Mica could say. She walked to the chair and set her bag and crystal kit on the ground. Buddha walked behind her curiously. She opened her tool kit of crystals and started rummaging through. He put his hand on top of hers to stop her and said, "I didn't call you here to heal me, I wanted to see your sweet face and tell you about your parents and prepare you for what is to come."

"But, you're going to die! I have to heal you," Mica said desperately.

"It's my time, Mica. I've missed you, give me a hug. I'm sorry, it's been so long, and I never told you I was your grandpa. It was for your own protection."

Mica buried her head in his chest and cried for what seemed like hours as he stroked her hair. At first, it felt like she was hugging a complete stranger, but then some part of her recognized his fatherly embrace, and she didn't ever want to be without him again.

"Shhhh, shhhh, everything will be all right. It's for the best and highest good of all, my darling granddaughter. You look just like your mother," he said pulling up her face to look at her and now a tear fell from his cheek.

"What happened to my parents, World Leader Mullen?"

"Please, Mica, call me grandpa, I've waited fourteen years for you to call me grandpa," he said with a big smile that reached ear to ear.

"Grandpa, grandpa, grandpa!" Mica giggled.

He laughed and then started coughing.

"OK, we don't have much more time, I need you to listen to everything I say, it's VERY important okay?"

Mica felt scared, but she nodded yes. Then, she wondered why she was really here.

"I don't believe in sugar coating things so I'm going to be honest and blunt. I was poisoned by Damian Black, who will be the New World Leader when I'm dead."

Mica's mouth opened in shock.

"Now listen and don't be scared. Mica, I'm so proud of you and I have a lot to tell you so just listen. Don't forget anything I say, and then you can talk. Okay?"

"OK," Mica said with tears streaming down her face.

"When you were born, your parents were so proud and happy and you were so tiny and beautiful. I loved your mother, my daughter, very much, but she was naïve. She knew you were special, yet she refused to believe that she or your father or you would be in any danger because of it. Damian Black is obsessed with anything out of the ordinary or magical.

He was in a village in England fifteen years ago seeking out a psychic renowned for her tarot card readings that foretold the future. She told him she saw him being the World Leader one day but that he would fail because a little girl being born the coming year and already in the womb would heal the people and all the lands. She said there would no longer be a need for a World Leader, because the people would be free from fear and no longer need ruling. She then gave him the last piece of information that led him to your mother. She said this little girl would be born of the current

World Leader's family. He knew right away that I was the one linked to you. So I had to take you from your mother and hide you with Priscilla, whom you call your Gran.

"Unfortunately I was too late to save your parents and Damian Black killed them in the hospital to make sure they wouldn't have another child to fulfill the prophecy. Your mother didn't approve of my plan, but she obliged. She let me publicly announce your death as a decoy, she held you for a few minutes before I took you away. I told her in a few months she could say they were adopting from another country and I could get you back to her. I was wrong; I let her be killed. Black found her an hour later and…" His voice wavered and so did Mica's mind at all the information.

He spoke up again before Mica could speak. "And so a prophecy was rumored through England. It goes like this; *She will save the world from the domes, healing her people and all the lands. She will free them from their plastic cage, and do all of this with her hands.* That prophecy is about you, Mica."

Mica's mouth had hung open for about two minutes now and so she slammed it shut. "Uh, what? I don't understand. I can't do that."

"Mica, you have a gift, you can heal anything that is hurt or sick or dying, ANYTHING!"

"I can't heal you!" she shot back.

"Because I want to go, it's my time. I'm needed elsewhere." He coughed some more. Mica saw that his energy had gotten very low, so she tried to send him some of her own from across the room, but it just came back. Silently she rubbed an amethyst in her pocket for strength.

"Mica, I promise you, if you go now and tell others you can heal the Earth and restore what global warming and ignorant humans did, they will believe you and follow you. You can heal the virus and save the human race. The Nanobots won't last. We have known for a while they are dying. Everyday the dome gets thinner and thinner as the Nanobots fail. People evolve Mica, everyone has a healer inside them now.

You must teach them how to access that inner healer. Gather everyone at sunrise on August 15th, in two months, and heal the Earth. YOU MUST or all hope is gone and Damian Black will start his plans of chaos, destruction, and power. He does not want peace in the domes, he wants survival of the fittest, and he will find a way to weed out the weak, old, and unwanted. The domes are getting crowded Mica, and there are not enough resources for another ten years. He will see to it that the desired ones survive and he'll dispose of the rest. If the domes can even hold long enough for him to begin his evil plan."

"What? I can't do that. Any plans he has, the countries Presidents would never let it happen!" Mica's mind was racing, her pulse quickened. She didn't understand why he was telling her all of this, why it was up to her to save everyone.

"I've seen his plans, Mica, that's why he's poisoned me. After I die he will be the new World Leader and eventually he'll start moving all the poor, slow, old, useless people into a dome and a fake "terrorist attack" is going to blow it up. It will be the next world war, Mica, and you must stop it. Gran will be in that dome, she's old. Mica, even the countries Presidents recognize that the domes are over crowded and running out of food, air and other necessities. People act crazy when they fear for their lives.

I think they will see logic in Damian Black's idea. They will act like animals and you must not let that happen. You are the only one who can fix everything. Heal the Earth and release the people from the domes. As you heal the Earth you heal the ID positive people. You will send a wave of healing energy that will engulf the planet. Humans can live as one again, in harmony."

"NO," Mica shrieked, "That's not fair! Stop him, expose him! I can't stop him and save the world, I'm fourteen years old! You're the World Leader, do something, call someone!"

"I did...I called you."

Mica dropped to her knees at the side of his bed. "This can't be," she exhaled. Her grandfather lifted her chin and stared into her welling eyes.

"Don't pretend you haven't always known you were going to do something big, something to make the world a better place." Mica tilted her head in sudden understanding. Hadn't she been saying that forever now? Telling the boy outside the domes she would figure out a way to make the world better. Is this what she'd meant? No, she never would have thought of this, but she couldn't watch people die and wars break out. The world had no need for such killing for no reason. No one should ever kill another human being. EVER.

Mica had always had an innate feeling of reincarnation. Like she had been here before. She honestly believed you never really died, as crazy as that sounds. So now she pondered how old she really must be. Technically she was fourteen, but she felt so much older, felt she had been at this for hundreds of years and now was her chance to use all of her wisdom and strength to help others. So in her mind, she pretended she was 800 years old, having the wisdom of many lifetimes of experience, and so she made up her mind to try.

"But how? So many people, so many domes, I'm the only one who can heal with crystals, how can other people just wake up one day and know how?"

"Mica, you don't heal with your crystals, you heal with your heart, your soul, and your hands. You charge up your crystals with healing light, so when the person holds it they feel better, but the crystals were only to get you comfortable with healing. They're just a safety net for you. Human's have evolved and have been healers for quite sometime. This ability lies dormant within them, they only need believe in order to heal. They will believe in themselves as they believe in you."

Mica looked at him. She did heal without the crystals sometimes, but it was hard for her to believe they weren't magical. They had always given her more power.

"Mica, do you see that dead plant?" He gestured to a small brown shrub in the corner, wilting in a blue pot.

"Yes." she sighed, not knowing where he was going with this. He was moving so fast, death, destruction, wars, no crystals, and now dead plants. His life force was shrinking.

"Heal it," he said, forcing out the words in his weakened state.

"What? It's a dead plant."

"Heal it, now," he said in a more commanding tone and coughed.

Mica had never tried to heal a plant before. What crystals would she use? On humans she knew which stones were good for which parts of the body. There was no plant healing stone! She was walking over to her crystal kit, thinking about how ridiculous this was, when he screamed at her.

"No! Are you listening to a word I'm saying? You don't need them, walk over and heal that plant!"

She felt small and mad; did he need to yell at her? This was stupid; she couldn't heal a dead plant and didn't want to, and especially not without her crystals!

She walked over to the plant and knelt in front of it. Then she looked over at him.

"Close your eyes, Mica, pretend it's Buddha when you found him half-dead behind the shop, you didn't have crystals then."

He was right, she didn't have crystals when she first healed Buddha, but she was so young then, and how did he know about that? She closed her eyes and imagined the plant's roots drinking water from the energy that she hoped was flowing out of her hands. She felt so lonely without the crystals for comfort. She imagined a bright gold energy, like the sun bathing the tops of the leaves. She barely heard her grandfather speaking. She slowly breathed and imagined a violet fire of pure healing light coming out of her mouth, and with each breath it wrapped itself around the plant. After ten minutes, she opened her eyes.

It was still brown and dead, but only for a second because, those were her negative thoughts tricking her; now it was green and tall and beautiful! She gasped out loud.

"You're ready," he said behind her.

She turned around to face her grandfather with a big smile. She'd done it, she'd healed a plant and now maybe she really could heal the Earth and the contaminated people. She stared at her grandpa in amazement, but he'd gone. His eyes had no sparkle.

Chapter Three
Dylan Pierce

He'd died with a smile on his face. He had no aura left. Her heart broke at the thought that she hadn't gotten to say, I love you, but then she felt a light breeze flutter her hair and she knew his spirit was saying good-bye and I love you too. She knew that his soul was now a part of the energy of the planet, and she would soon use that energy to heal it. She cried over his body for a long time. It was important to shed tears when you felt them under your skin. She knew bottling up sadness was bad for her, so she released it all. Most of the people she'd healed of cancer had gotten the disease from bottling their tears, their sadness, and fears. She thought she and her grandfather would have more time together. She wanted to ask about her parents, but now he was gone, and Gran wasn't here, and she literally felt the weight of the world on her shoulders. In his hands was a package that he'd been holding the whole time. Mica examined the tag hanging off its side,

My Dear Mica, it read. Just before she could open it, the monk burst into the room. Seeing the dead World Leader he recoiled.

"Men have just driven through the gates," he mumbled, "the men your grandfather warned me about. We must sneak you through the secret tunnel and back to the airport."

"Take that package and open it later," he added.

She didn't waste a moment, Mica kissed her grandfathers cheek and then grabbed the package in a hurry. The monk wrestled with her bags, leading her to the far end of the room and a painting of the Buddha. He rubbed the paintings belly and the wall began to open, revealing a dark tunnel made of stone. The monk looked at Mica and smiled, "The secret tunnel," he motioned her inside and lit a torch that hung on the wall.

Mica set Buddha down and he immediately began sniffing the ground.

"Follow me, this tunnel runs a mile underground to a small dirt field where we can take a car to the airport. I suspect your driver tipped off Damian Black and his men. I had bad feelings about him, so I'm not sure who you can trust."

Mica slowed her pace a little at the mention that Damian Black was looking for her. Already? He killed her parents, should she go back and confront him? Yeah right, Mica thought.

"Well, apparently I can trust you."

The man looked back at her still jogging and smiled, he was panting and Mica guessed he didn't exercise much and this was probably very straining. Mica never considered herself a claustrophobic person, but with the tunnel inches from her head and only the small torch to light her way, she found it hard to breathe. She was relived when she saw light ahead and they neared the end of the tunnel. They reached the outside and approached an old vehicle. It was a large rusty truck with empty wooden animal crates in the back.

"I haven't driven for thirty-five years so if you pray, now would be a good time," the monks face was serious and set in determination.

"Umm, well, maybe we should call someone. Besides, this doesn't look like it's been converted which would be illegal to drive." Mica was nervous about driving with this old man who had forgotten how, in a car that still ran on gas.

The monk smiled. "It's diesel, I'll probably be fined or arrested, but it will be an adventure. Come on, climb in," he smiled again, like a teenager on the verge of doing something crazy. Mica stifled a laugh, in spite of her grandfather dying and her being chased by Damian Black, a monk seeking an adventure was slightly comical.

"You're not afraid of jail?" She asked.

"What is jail to a disciplined monk who prays all day in a small room?"

She picked up Buddha and climbed in the truck, the seat gave up a puff of dust as she sat down. The monk held the keys tightly in prayer clasped hands, mumbling under his breath. He turned the key and the engine rumbled to life, almost as loud as the jet engine, Mica thought. Black smoke spat out the tailpipe and they were off.

"It's all coming back to me, we're fine." The monk assured Mica.

Mica was clenching the seat trying not to throw up; the truck was lurching over the uneven ground making it's way to the highway. The monk was leaning into the bumps with his body and jerking the wheel in the process. After they turned onto the highway, Mica breathed a little easier.

"You should open that gift now, before you get to the plane." The monk said.

Mica invited Buddha onto her lap and opened the wrapping. The second the corner of the lid came off the box, a vibrating blue and silver light spread out. Mica got nervous and excited at the same time. Once the lid was completely off she picked up what looked like a large heavy solid egg, but it was a stone. It had two colors, deep red and dark grey, swirled over the smooth surface. Just holding the heavy stone made her feel dizzy, for it held so much energy within it. There was a letter underneath the egg stone in the box. She opened it and read.

My Angel,

If we do not have time to talk about this gift, I want to explain it to you. Burn this afterwards. You are holding a Shiva Lingham Stone from the sacred Narmada River that flows in India. You must take very special care of it and never let anyone else have it. As you may feel, this stone is full of energy, but when it's wet, it changes the frequency of your DNA to transport you into other dimensions and worlds. In these worlds your power to see auras will be different because your frequency is different. Just focus your intention on what you want in a world, and it will take you to the world that has the most of that quality.

Mica set down the letter at this point and wondered if maybe in his poisoned state, her grandfather had gone a bit insane. Other worlds? DNA? Frequency? It all sounded crazy, But the letter was dated two years ago… She swallowed hard and kept reading.

Everything in the world runs off of a certain frequency. The air, the water, even humans are made up of a certain vibration and frequency. Scientifically, if you could change a person's vibration to that of another world they would become invisible to this world and exist in that one, but this is not scientific, it's magical. This stone has been in our family for generations. Your great-great-grandfather pulled it out of the river himself. He too had the healing gift and a fondness for stones. He was a quantum physicist and understood that other worlds existed and it was just a matter of changing your frequency to see them. He brought the stone home and put his hands on it everyday, flooding it, and charging it with energy, with the intention of changing its properties. He wanted to see if he could think it into being different, and he did. After a year, he made it what it is today. A universal traveling device that cuts through all worlds, all levels, and dimensions. Mica, you MUST promise not to let anyone see, touch, or know about this unless you trust them with your very soul. We don't want someone getting it and destroying it.

The reason they would destroy it is because your genius great-great-grandfather made it so that it only takes people into other worlds that have a true heart to help the planet for the best and highest good. So, to a person with ill intentions it would just be a wet rock. To stop the good from prevailing they might destroy it. But to you, my darling, it's your destiny. So go now, my brave granddaughter, and speak your truth. Tell people around the world, that with your help, humanity can restore Mother Earth to her peaceful and pure state. I love you very much; your parents loved you more than I could ever write down. Good Luck, Mica. You won't need it. You're the ONE.

P.S. Look for signs that the universe is moving in your favor. If you need help say what you need out loud and watch it appear.

ALL MY LOVE,

Grandpa

    The monk was whistling happily and completely unaware that he was driving like a lunatic. Mica read the note two more times and burned it with matches that were in the package, tossing the flaming remnants out the window. Absent-mindedly she thought of how bad the smoke was for the environment, but saw no other way. She slipped the Shiva Lingham Stone in her purple velvet bag. The monk exited the highway and they were approaching the airport. He parked in front of the private jet hangar and stopped the engine. Suddenly, Mica knew this was goodbye and felt lonely.

"Mica Moon, it has been a pleasure. I can now say that I truly helped make the world a better place by helping you to safety."

Mica arched her eyebrows at the odd name he called her. "Mica Moon?"

"Oh, your grandfather didn't tell you? I suppose he thought he had more time. You are the daughter of Amber and Luka Moon. Your real name is Mica Moon. Foster, was just a cover up to elude Damian Black. Now that you are on your true path, I think Mica Moon is appropriate."

He reached across the seat and placed a finger on Mica's forehead. "Bless you child," Buddha barked loudly making Mica and the monk jump. "Bless you too, sweet Buddha." The monk said touching Buddha's forehead. And with that Mica jumped down from the truck with her bags and set off for the jet.

Her head was reeling; she felt like a machine on autopilot. A dying man had given her a task, and now she was like a robot trying to figure out the first step toward completing it.

Mica thought of the last words in her grandfathers note, *If you need help say what you need out loud and watch it appear.*

"Say what I want out loud? I want help!" she shrieked. "I don't want to do this alone, I want someone I can trust, who is special like me and will never leave my side no matter what!!!" Tears were streaming down her face onto her lips, and they tasted salty. She needed sweet right now not salt, she was mad at her own tears. She stood there feeling stupid that no one had appeared after she said she needed help, and so she stepped onto the jet so she could try to save the world. Alone!

Far away in London, Dylan Pierce shot out of bed. He grabbed his dream journal and started writing things down feverishly. Afterwards, he set the book aside and took a deep breath. This dream was unlike any other he had ever had. The girl, her white hair and silver blue eyes, the clock in the shop at the airport, the glimpses of her talking to a dying man, talking to the World Leader.

Having prophetic dreams was a blessing and a curse. A blessing when the dreams delivered good news or helped save someone from danger, but when you had to tell someone they had cancer or that they are going to die, it's completely different.

But this was a prophetic dream about him. He had never had one of his dreams about himself. So he knew this must be serious. He silently told himself that he needed to do everything in the dream. The dream was a gift to help him stay on his life path, he knew it! This was the road he should take, he always knew he would be part of something big, but he never thought it would happen like this. He put on the clothes from his dream, packed his red backpack, pulled the green crystal from his pillowcase and tied it in his long bohemian brown hair, and then he snuck out of the orphanage window to meet the girl of his dreams, literally, and help her with her colossal task.

Mica's pilot had just landed in London at Heathrow airport to stock up on things and re-power the electric jet's battery. Mica was planning to stay on the plane, but she had never been to London before and she wanted to look around even if it was just at the airport. Maybe she would hear lots of funny accents or see someone dressed differently. She told the pilot she would be back in ten minutes, and she left Buddha on the plane. The pilot tried to make her stay, saying it wasn't safe but she ran out anyway; she needed to get away and think about her plan of action.

She was walking along the row of shops inside, pondering about how she was going to go about healing the entire world, when she suddenly saw a bright, large, colorful aura over one entire shop. It was ten feet high and thirty feet wide and she was spellbound as she made her way into the bookstore. Mica loved to read, but normally a bookstore wouldn't give off that much energy. She scanned the shop half-expecting to see hundreds of people in deep prayer or something serious, which would radiate such beautiful, intense energy, and then she saw him.

A boy about her age stood against a bookcase with long, shoulder-length, brown hair, some pieces were braided and he wore a torn red scarf in his hair like a headband. His shoulders were broad, and he was tall and slender but muscular. His face was smooth and almost feminine in its beauty. He had the largest aura Mica had ever seen. He was leaned against the shelf, sifting through a book. He had on a white, long-sleeved collared shirt with the sleeves rolled up, showcasing all of his jewelry. He wore over twenty bracelets on one arm, some with little bells on them, and some ragged strips of leather and beads; he also had a few rings on his fingers, some as big as his knuckle. He wore a brown leather vest and Mica thought he looked like a pirate. Then something in his hair caught her eye. It was a green crystal, a very rare moldavite shard hanging from a leather strip in one of his braids. She walked up to him scanning his aura. He was honest and kind, but there was something mysterious about him. He had some sadness in his heart that one only acquires after a tragedy or loss.

"Where did you get that crystal?" Mica blurted out in amazement.

Dylan slammed the book shut and whipped his head up wearing a smile looking Mica straight in the face. His eyes startled her; they looked like they had contained lighting bolts right inside them. They were mint-green with flecks of bright yellow. He squinted like a cat. She stared at him, waiting for him to speak, realizing she couldn't look away from those electric eyes.

"Well, first of all I'm not a pirate. I'm a gypsy," he said smiling. Mica recoiled, wondering if she voiced her thought out loud.

"The crystal was my father's; he was a gypsy too. His great-grandfather retrieved it from Czechoslovakia after a gigantic meteorite the size of Buckingham palace blasted into the ground. Some say it's an alien rock." He smirked at her expression of amazement. She was exactly like the girl in his dream.

"Really? Because I collect crystals, and I've never seen one of those, only in books. It's beautiful and very rare."

"Yeah, but he and my mother died seven years ago, and it's all I have left of my family." Now his eyes were downcast.

Mica scanned his aura; he was telling the truth. "I'm sorry to hear that, how did they die? My parents are dead also." She added sadly.

"They were killed in Darfur, for protesting against the genocide when I was seven. Even though World Leader Mullen declared peace in the domes, they were still killing women and children for not believing certain things. My parents left me with my grandmother in a gypsy camp and went to Africa to try and stop the murders. They were trampled to death by African military after their peaceful demonstration was raided. My grandmother died the next year and so the English government put me in an orphanage in London."

"Oh, I'm sorry." Mica said. Dylan knew from his dream that this was all a part of her trusting him. So far this was exactly like his dream.

Dylan stuck out his hand. "I'm Dylan, and I'm here to help you, Mica." He took her hand gently, knowing what would happen.

Mica looked at him with disbelief as he took her hand, she felt a shock run through her body. She jerked away and stared at him.

"What was that? You playing some kind of joke? What do you mean you're here to help me? You don't even know me. How do you know my name?"

"I know I can trust you, because you're different, like me, so I'm just going to tell you the truth OK?"

"OK." Mica was stunned and a little scared. She rubbed her hand; it felt as though electricity had zapped her. But her grandfather's letter echoed in her mind. *(Look for signs that the universe is moving in your favor, say what you want out loud and watch it appear.)*

"I have psychic dreams," Dylan said letting the words linger in the air. Mica was speechless; but she didn't laugh so he went on.

"This crystal was handed down to me because I hold the gift of many in my family. We are seers. I put the crystal in my pillow or tie it in my hair and I see future events in my dreams or my crystal speaks into my ear. I saw this. I saw you being drawn into this shop; I saw the clock being this time and us having this same conversation. I even saw us being shocked when we touched although I don't know what that's about. Then I was shown something else entirely. I was shown you talking to the World Leader. I saw you heal that plant with your hands and I know the task you have been given, so I'm here to help you. I heard you ask for help and I woke up. So here I am." His face was dead serious.

Mica was shocked. She had asked for help but hadn't actually expected any, especially not in the form of a young psychic gypsy boy who looked like a pirate. She didn't know if she could trust him.

The crystal in Dylan's ear whispered softly, as it sometimes did. *Prove to her she can trust you*, it said

"You can trust me, Mica. I want to help the world just like you do. I want to make my parents proud and do something positive for the world and I can't do it alone."

Mica wondered if he could read her mind. She scanned his aura, it was pure and golden and white with baby blue. He was speaking from his heart, and she knew he was just like her and wanted a better place for everyone to live in.

"Okay, you can come, but it's not going to be easy. It's dangerous, I've already had to travel through a secret tunnel to escape bad people and I don't even know if we can do it," Mica said being honest.

"We can do it," Dylan said with a smile.

Mica knew right then that she would never be alone in the world again. She knew Dylan understood what it was like to be different and that he wouldn't leave her side. Her cheeks turned red at the thought and she turned and started walking towards the plane.

Dylan followed her in silence. He marveled at the way she carried herself; she looked about thirteen or fourteen years old but she acted much more mature. He saw her in his dream, healing that plant and he wondered what else she could do. He had never seen someone with such fair skin and silvery hair. And those eyes, those ice blue eyes made her look like an angel. She wore crystal bracelets and necklaces and walked with a bit of a strut. He thought she would fit right in with his gypsy clan. Just as they stepped onto the plane, Buddha came running towards them.

"This is Buddha," Mica said holding up the small fluffy dog.

Dylan reached out his hand and Buddha smelled it for twenty seconds before licking it, Dylan laughed and picked him up. He was light in his hands maybe six or seven pounds. "Hi there, Buddha." Buddha barked happily.

"Why did you name him Buddha? Buddha is a fat man in the Buddhist religion, you know."

Mica laughed good and hard at that.

"I know. Well, I rescued him from death and he was so small and frail I wanted to give him a big strong name that everyone would like and that would signify authority. Who doesn't like the Buddha? You can rub his belly for luck and," she paused, "I dunno; it just fits, but I don't think the Buddhists would like you calling their Buddha fat." They both laughed now freely.

Mica watched him play with Buddha and wondered if their meeting meant they were supposed to start her plan right away.

Two months wasn't very long, and while they were in London, it might be nice to spread the word about healing the planet, before they got all the way to New York where she intended to go. The more people the better. Part of her was too nervous to start, but she knew she must.

"Dylan, do you know many people here? People that want to help cure the contaminated ones, to reverse global warming, people that want a natural free world? We need to start recruiting people to join us."

"I know of the gypsy camp about two hours outside of London in Brighton. I haven't been there since my grandmother died but I'm sure they would listen to what you had to say."

"Well, then I think before we leave for New York, we should talk to them. We must start now or we won't be able to get enough people to heal the planet in two months."

Dylan smiled, marveling at her courageousness, he had met a worthy friend. The gypsies would surely listen to a girl with the courage of a lion.

"Then let's do this," Dylan said.

Mica packed a bag with the Shiva Lingham stone, some sandwiches and dry food for Buddha. She was hesitant to leave her crystal case behind, but trusted her grandfather, he'd said she'd no longer needed the crystals to heal. She spoke with the pilot, who reluctantly agreed to stay behind and wait for them.

They took the train, which was electric, since all fuel driven transportation was outlawed. Only a few government-issued electric taxis were aloud to ride and it cost a fortune. On the train ride Mica, briefed Dylan on everything, the task ahead, her power to see peoples aura's and heal them. In turn, Dylan told her of his dreams and how he can predict certain events and even keep them from happening. The only thing Mica didn't tell him was about the Shiva Lingham.

When they arrived in Brighton, they were at the very edge of the dome. There was an ocean right outside the dome, Dylan told Mica, but the domes cut it off because the water was sick and dangerous from the global warming which had killed most of the sea life and plagued the water with disease. A few streets from the train stop, it seemed as though they were in another world. There were long winding cobblestone streets and lots of people. Dylan brought her to the end of one of the roads and paused.

"Is this it?" Mica said looking around at the row of shops.

"There used to be an alley here, it led to a thicket of bushes and it was just beyond that."

"Are you sure it was here?"

"I'm sure. My mother would get me ice cream from the shop right there. They must have built up new shops since then." He pointed to an old ice cream shop and Mica could see it made him sad to explore the memories of his mother. Suddenly Mica felt a pull in her chest, forcing her to walk further down the street.

"Where are we going?" Dylan asked.

"I don't know. I feel pulled, like someone's energy is guiding me." Buddha barked and followed them down the street.

Mica felt the energy grow stronger and tug her to the left. She followed like a puppet out of control, down an alley, behind the buildings. "Is this normal? Does this usually happen?" Dylan was a little worried about who was drawing them in.

"No, I've never had this happen before, but it doesn't feel bad, the energy feels okay."

"Oh, OK." Dylan puffed up his chest and prepared himself for anything. They were walking down an alley with large bushes on the right. Suddenly an old mess of a woman with raven black hair jumped out and grabbed Mica and Dylan and pulled them into the bushes out of sight.

Chapter Four
The Gypsies

Once inside, Dylan realized this was it, they were in the hidden gypsy camp. It looked so familiar. Mica clung to his arm, her eyes closed, afraid they were being kid-napped.

"Open your eyes, Mica dear, I'm not going to hurt you." The black-haired woman said as she cackled wildly. Mica opened her eyes.

"Who are you?" Dylan and Mica said in unison.

"I'm Gretta Grimes. I'm here to help you find the place, you were havin a bit o' trouble weren't ya?" Gretta's accent was thick and Irish; there was no mistaking it.

Mica scanned her aura, her third eye chakra, was huge the size of a soccer ball, and it was deep purple with magenta swirls in it. She had silver energy chords going from her brain into Dylan's head, so she must be psychic. Mica had heard about such people and knew there were many fakes, but this woman must really be one, with an aura like that.

"Could you please not read our minds, its rude!" Mica blurted out in a snappy voice, not wanting Gretta to know about the plan or the Shiva Lingham. As she said it the silvery chords to Dylan's brain snapped and rolled back into Gretta's head.

Gretta's eyes perked up. "I didn't mean to be rude, honey, it's all I know," she said and then she fell to her knees.

"You can see my abilities, you really are the one, and you've come to save us!" Gretta gasped enthusiastically. "I've waited so long to meet you, child!"

"I've gathered four hundred gypsies from all over England and Ireland to hear you speak and teach us what must be done," Gretta said and bowed.

Whoa, she really must know everything, Mica thought. She felt really uncomfortable with this woman on her knees and wished she would stand up. As soon as she thought it, the woman stood up, smiling.

"Four hundred people? Ummm well, yeah, that's a good start, I was thinking it would be more like twenty," Mica said in a nervous voice.

"Four hundred is perfect! The more the merrier. We can do this Mica!" Dylan said enthusiastically.

"I know we can," Mica said defiantly, not wanting to sound scared.

Gretta took Mica's hands and looked her in the eyes.

"Mica, I'm the one who made the prophesy about you dear. I gave Damian Black that Tarot reading many years ago, and it was me who led him to your parents. I'm so sorry, child, please forgive me. Your daddy was a gypsy and I raised him like my own child; he would be so proud of you. I'm so ashamed," Gretta said, crying freely.

"My parents were gypsies?" Mica said in disbelief.

"I knew it, I knew you had gypsy blood in you!" Dylan said with a triumphant smile.

"Your father was, yes, but your mother was a pretty little American thing who lived in London every summer and caught your father's eye." Gretta said.

"Luka was in town one day when he was about seventeen, and he saw your mother walking out of a bookstore. He knew from that day on he would love her forever. He walked right up to her and said, 'Hi I'm your soul mate, Luka.'" Gretta howled in laughter.

"Your mother, of course, stalked off thinking he was loony, but your dad came back to the village bookshop everyday until he saw her again, and soon they were deep in love. Your father, like you, had a fondness for gemstones. He gave your mother a heart-shaped rose quartz necklace to signify their love." Gretta pulled something out of her pocket and dangled it in front of Mica. It was the necklace. "May you wear it and always know that your parents loved you very much."

Mica took the necklace and was jolted by it's energy force. She felt her heart spill over with affection and tenderness and felt complete and whole. Dylan knew from Mica's eye's what she was feeling. In fact, her eyes seemed so familiar, that he wondered if he hadn't seen her before, before the airport, before the dreams. She looked up at him and his cheeks flushed.

"Your mother and father dated for a year, and then he moved to America to be with her and later, start a family. Amber and Luka both loved crystals, which is why they named you Mica; they'd both be so proud of you. They wanted the world to be better for you than it is. Your grandfather was World Leader, and Damian came to see me and I was reading for him, not knowing how evil he was, and it all just slipped out. This necklace came to me in the mail, because I requested it from your grandfather, knowing one day I would see you again. Please,"

Gretta, paused, crying, "Forgive me, so I may die one day in peace."

Mica squeezed the woman's hands and said one of the hardest things of her life. "Everything happens for a reason, I forgive you." I forgive you for killing my parents, Mica thought. Then she was nervous that Gretta had picked up on the thought.

Dylan felt awkward witnessing this personal moment. He decided to break the silence. "Ok then, ready to do this?" he asked nervously, noticing the people across the hill gathering around. Mica slipped the rose quartz heart around her neck and smiled at Dylan.

And with that, Gretta lead the way and Mica felt the pressure. How had everything happened so fast? Was she ready? Could she really do this? Mica took a big deep breath, and she, Dylan, Gretta, and Buddha walked over the hill towards the mass of murmuring people staring at them.

The gypsy camp was an adornment of RVs, striped silk tents, and exotic flowers. There was a makeshift platform nestled in the center of the camp and Mica walked up to it. She looked back at Dylan who nodded in encouragement. She said the first thing that flew out of her mouth, addressing over four hundred people.

"We're all going to die!" she screamed. People seemed shocked; they were looking at Gretta and murmuring and started stepping back to walk away.

"Wait! I mean with the old World Leader dead, a new leader will rise." Her voice was loud and carried through the crowd; she took a deep breath, regaining her composure and went on, "If we keep living like this, trapped in the domes, we will run out of food and energy and we won't survive. We don't have to live like this any more! Humans have evolved; we can heal Mother Earth and reverse global warming, we can heal the contaminated and finally live in a free world." She let those words linger.

"In two full moons' time, in the morning of the rising sun on August 15th in America, I will lay my hands on the Earth and think of love, peace, harmony, and gratitude and send my healing energy to the very core of it. If enough people do it, too, then the Earth can be healed, and we won't have to live in the domes any longer. We won't have to worry about breathing sick air, or eating bad food or getting the ID virus. We won't have to fear the depleting Nanobots that threaten to diminish our shelter. These Nanobots are just microscopic computers not magic. Their time is up, their motherboards are frying and then we are on our own! But if you help me, the sun will nourish our skin, instead of damaging it, the people on the outside will walk amongst us again, healthy. The world will be free, but you must believe in me, in what I'm telling you. You are all great healers, and so am I." Micas hands were shaking.

"Prove it! Prove you can heal the Earth!" a man in the crowd shouted.

Mica's heart raced, they weren't believing in her. Her grandpa said they would. She stood there not knowing what to do. Suddenly, from behind the crowd, Mica saw a bright golden thread coming from the sky and dripping down into a dead tree like syrup. Mica started walking towards it before she even knew what she was going to do. The crowd parted. She looked deep into the ground and saw that the roots were not dead yet, they had a faint blazing golden aura to them. This tree was alive.

All the people started whispering, wondering what she was doing. This tree was much larger than the dead plant she'd healed in front of her grandpa. Mica looked at Dylan; he smiled brightly. Mica walked to the foot of the tree and started rubbing her palms together. People were whispering more now, but Mica tuned them out. In her head all was silent and she knelt on the cold Earth and laid the palms of her hands flat on the ground four inches from the trunk. Mica imagined all the light from the roots growing upward into the trunk itself and out onto the branches, forming bright green leaves. Mica saw golden light coming down from her hands and into the tree. She hoped with all her soul that the tree was accepting her light. She breathed slowly, and kept feeding the tree with light, but it was sucking it out of her so fast she wasn't sure if she would have enough energy.

Then she felt two hands on her back and a massive amount of light flew from her hands and illuminated the entire tree. People gasped in shock as the dead brown tree turned green, and even Mica felt shock as bright green leaves grew out of the brittle dead branches.

The hands fell away from her back, and she stood up, turning quickly to see no one standing within ten feet of her. Chills ran down her spine, and people started clapping and cheering and kneeling before Mica. Some of the women were crying and the men gasped in shock. Mica didn't know what to say. They seemed to be waiting for her to talk, but her mind was still on whose hands were on her back. Just behind the people Dylan jumped on the make-shift stage and spoke in a powerful voice.

"There! You have your proof. Now will you help us to heal the world?"

There was a small moment of silence before everyone cried out, "YES! YES!" and cheered.

Mica found her voice and spoke one last time.

"Tell everyone you know of what you have seen here today, tell them that when the time comes, on August 15th with the rising sun, they must drop to the Earth and lay their hands on the soil with love. Just feel love and appreciation for the Earth and all that she gives us, think of how happy you would be in a world with no domes, no viruses, no pollution, think of how it would feel to be FREE, to live in a freeworld!" Mica screamed the last two words with all her might, joining them as one. She wanted people to understand how important this was.

The entire crowd was talking loudly saying things like, "Yes, We will tell everyone we know, and you can count on us," and they chanted, "Freeworld! Freeworld! Freeworld!"

As Mica and Dylan said goodbye to Gretta she assured them the gypsies would spread the world about the healing and they made there way back to the train in silence.

Back at the private jet, the pilot was sleeping, Mica and Dylan were exhausted too, so they shut and locked the hatch and fell quickly asleep with Buddha at their feet. When they awoke they were landing on a tarmac. The pilot came over the loud speaker,

"We have arrived at JFK airport in New York City."

The plane was pulling into the private garage when Buddha started growling. The stone in Dylan's ear was vibrating and giving him gooseflesh. "Buddha be quiet, it's ok," Mica said.

"Um, Mica, I have a bad feeling," Dylan said.

"About what?" Mica asked. His face was distraught.
The crystal in Dylan's ear spoke, *Exit out the emergency hatch now!*

"Grab your stuff! We'll leave through the emergency hatch," Dylan said sternly, while shoving Micas things into a bag and latching her case of gemstones. Mica didn't question him and grabbed Buddha. They were opening the rear left side, emergency exit hatch of the plane, just as the pilot stepped out of the flight deck in front. As they dropped onto the cement, Mica stopped dead in her tracks peering around to the front of the plane while backing under it, to hide.

"I'm seeing a ghost," she said in a wavering voice.

"What? Come on, let's go!" Dylan urged.

He turned to see what she was looking at and saw a man in a dark black suit and red fedora hat standing at the main hatch, talking to the pilot in a fury.

"Let's go! That man is bad!!!" Dylan screamed feeling the intensity of the pilot's conversation with the man.

They started running out onto the tarmac away from the men, Dylan carrying his backpack and the silver case. Mica had Buddha in one hand and dragged her tan duffle bag with the other; purple purse slung across her neck.

"You saw him? You saw the ghost?" Mica asked, breathing deeply.

"He's not a ghost, he's alive and real just like you and me. What makes you think he was a ghost?" Dylan was breathing hard too, trying to figure out where they should go. Mica stopped.

"Dylan, everyone I have ever met has had an aura, a life force, a glow about them that makes them who they are, the energy of their soul, like a spiritual finger print."

"OK," Dylan said not knowing where this was going, but wanting her to move along.

"That man had no aura. He had no life force. He has NO soul, that man was Damian Black," those last words gave Dylan chills.

"Well then we better run faster. That man just became the new World Leader," Dylan said as he opened the gate through which they would escape.

"Do you have any money?"

"Thirty-four dollars," Mica said proudly.

"Great," Dylan said sarcastically. He only had fifty. Eighty-four dollars was not going to get them far in New York City.

They walked out to the terminal-parking garage and found their way to an underground train stop. It didn't matter where it went, he just wanted to get on it.

They rode the train for a long time, changing trains twice before they decided they were far enough away from the man in the dark suit. They got off at 33rd Street and walked a few blocks until Mica saw a 24-hour grocery on Lexington and 34th. They went inside to get some food.

"Excuse me, what time is it?" Dylan asked

"One a.m., you buy food?" the Asian man asked angrily.

"Yeah, yeah we're going to buy food." Dylan said sleepily.

After paying $20 for some fruit and two sandwiches, they left. Mica thought it odd that the man wasn't concerned about two kids out alone at one a.m., but she guessed that in New York that wasn't uncommon.

"We need to find somewhere safe to sleep," Dylan said, feeling jet lagged. He looked across the street at the Murray Hill apartments and got an idea.

"Stay here with our stuff, I'll be right back," he said grabbing Buddha and walking off.

"Wait, what? Why are you taking Buddha?"

He stopped and looked back at her "Trust me," he said. His dark hair was in such contrast to his green eyes. Mica wondered if he had done this sort of thing before, he was so mysterious. She wondered about the life he had lived up until she met him. Dylan strutted into the apartments' front desk yawning.

"Damn dog has to pee every ten minutes," he said to the doorman walking up to the elevator.

"Oh, ah, yeah, what apartment are you from?" The elevator doors closed before the man could finish and Dylan hoped he wouldn't come looking for him. It was late and the man appeared to have been sleeping. He got off at the 2nd floor and headed toward the emergency exit door. There was no alarm. "You're a good boy, Buddha," Dylan said petting him. He entered the staircase and walked down to the street level and opened the door.

"Pssst, over here," he said, smiling at Mica waiting for her to recognize the brilliance of his plan.

"Took you long enough, I'm freezing out here! I don't understand why they still allow it to be cold when they can control the climate in the domes." She walked into the stairwell and took Buddha back to pet him. "So what now?" she asked.

"Well, I think we should go up to about the eighth floor, just in case the front desk guy knows I got off on two and starts looking."

Once they got settled on the steps of the eighth floor, Mica was wide-awake. She laid her head on her canvas bag. Dylan sprawled out on the platform next to her.

"I didn't get very good sleep on the plane, so I'm going to bed," Dylan said.

"OK."

"Dylan?"

"Yeah?" Dylan said groggily

"Thanks for finding me, I don't think I could have done this alone."

Dylan opened his eyes, "I just answered your call," he said smiling and drifted off to sleep.

Mica sat there in the darkness for a long while, petting Buddha, listening to the sound of Dylan's breathing. She was trying to process what happened at the airport. She had seen Damian Black on TV a few times because he was the American Leader, but she didn't see auras on TV so she assumed he had one. Seeing him in person confirmed everything her grandpa had told her. That man was impossible, to have no aura, but be alive and now they were hiding out from him and the dangerous city in a stairwell. That was a good idea, she thought. If Dylan weren't here she didn't know where she would be right know. After a while, Dylan's rhythmic breathing tranquilized Mica into sleep.

Dylan woke up first and stared at Mica, she twitched her nose the slightest bit when she slept. She started to stir, so he jumped up and started gathering their things.

"Good morning, Dylan, good morning Buddha," she laughed as Buddha jumped on her and licked her face.

"Let's catch a train somewhere and see if we can't find someone to tell our crazy story to." Dylan said, mocking their situation.

They both laughed at that. Because it was crazy wasn't it? *Hi my name's Mica, and I'm going to heal the entire Earth in one day with your help!* hah! It definitely sounded crazy.

They got on the number 6 train and went to central park. In Sedona there were no trains. Everyone rode bikes or electric cars. Being from London, Dylan knew how to get around using the subway and Mica was glad he was there to guide her.

Dogs weren't allowed on the train, so they had to hide Buddha in Mica's purple velvet bag. But he kept peeking his head out in excitement and nervousness at being underground and moving so fast.

They exited the train and made their way out onto the street. They were a few yards from the Central park opening when the safety alarms went off, every streetlight flickered and the sirens resounded. A cheery female voice came over a loudspeaker and echoed on the cold sidewalk, "Please put on your safety masks, a contamination has been detected." Dylan scrambled through his backpack for his government issued mask and Mica dropped everything looking for hers as well. She stuck Buddha inside her coat zipping it up while attaching her mask. A red rain-like mist fell from the sky. Disinfectant. It hit her skin and clothes turning clear. She was safe and Dylan was safe as well.

A woman a few feet up started shrieking, her skin was blue. She had been contaminated having the classic ID positive reaction to the disinfectant. Men in HAZMAT suits appeared out of a black van taking the woman, Mica knew the woman would join the rest outside. She would face her certain death. The van wheeled off before Mica could even think about healing the woman.

"Contamination contained, you may remove your masks." The polite female voice offered.

Dylan looked at Mica, "That was close." They shrugged off the incident and entered the park, which was more like a city in itself, so big, so many bridges and horses and lakes. They bought hotdogs from a street vendor, and then sat down and enjoyed the food, basking in the sunlight. Buddha ran around wildly, it had been days since he had been on a walk.

Mica and Dylan were discussing what they should do next when the crystal in Dylan's ear whispered something and he glanced around nervously, just in time to notice two girls ducking behind a tree. "Mica, someone is following us or stalking us or something." He pointed to the tree and Mica saw two auras exactly the same in every way, but one had the purplish magenta third eye like Gretta. Mica got up and Dylan seized her arm.

"No, lets go. They're following us," Dylan warned.

"It's OK, I think they're here to help. I'll be right back."

Dylan tensed his body at her unwillingness to listen to him, she was too naive, he thought, and hoped it wouldn't get them into trouble later on. Then again she could read people better than he could and she saw their energy for who they truly were, so maybe it was all right to trust her judgment. He just wasn't sure yet.

She walked over to the tree and the girls started walking away.

"Hey wait! It's OK, let's talk," Mica shouted.

Both of the girls whipped around, and Mica saw that they were identical twins. They each wore what looked like school uniforms, a white blouse and navy blue skirt. They had dark brown straight hair and almond-shaped brown eyes. They made their way back up to her, and the one on the left spoke.

"I'm Chloe, and this is my sister Nadia. She has visions which I think are stupid, but she wants me to tell you that because she had a vision about you last night." She paused, looking at her sister giving her a nasty look. Mica noticed the deep red jealousy in Chloe's aura when she spoke, in contrast to Nadia's pink, loving compassion for her sister.

In the middle of Nadia's forehead was a rich purple spinning wheel of energy. Mica called it a chakra, because Gran had taught her chakra meant wheel in Sanskrit and every person had seven of these colored wheels in their auras. Usually Mica tuned them out and only focused on the aura but Nadia's third eye chakra, the one associated with psychic abilities, was glistening and illuminated and Mica wondered how many intuitive people she was going to meet on this journey. Instead of sucking information out of her brain like Gretta, Mica saw that Nadia was directly connected to her sister by a white wispy chord going from one brain to the other. Then she had many little white chords waving in what seemed like unseen water picking up thoughts all around her. They seemed to share these thoughts through the large white chord.

"Okay," Mica said, "what visions has she gotten about me?"

"Just that you need to come to our house, our mom is at work and we ditched school because we have to help you." She said this with annoyance like she didn't really want to help at all. Nadia however smiled and nodded.

"Thank you very much. Does Nadia talk?" Mica inquired.

"No! And it doesn't matter, I know what she wants to say. I guess the boy can come too," Chloe said, waving her hand as if Mica were a servant and referring to Dylan who was standing behind Mica. Mica wondered if she had servants at home and this was how she spoke to them. Chloe waited a few seconds and turned up her nose and started walking away.

Nadia waved them to follow.

"Dylan, let's go!" Mica shouted back at him.

Dylan looked at her, alarmed, but followed anyway. They took another train in total silence, fearing Chloe would act as a drill sergeant if they spoke out of turn. Once they all arrived at the girls apartment, Chloe told them both how much they smelled and how dirty they were. So Mica took a shower in their mother's bathroom and Dylan showered in the girls'. Nadia gave Mica a sweater, because all Mica had brought were Arizona warm weather clothes, nothing for the icy cold New York weather. Chloe didn't give her anything; she just stayed in her room. When Mica came out all dressed cleanly; she found Nadia playing with Buddha laughing and giggling. Mica sat down beside her.

"I do talk," Nadia whispered, "my sister gets jealous that I have visions and she doesn't, so she talks to feel special."

Just then the door flew open.

"So what do we do now?" Chloe asked Nadia in a rude tone, cutting off their conversation.

Mica sat in amazement, watching as Nadia fed all of her thoughts through this white cord, which looked like a bulging sausage expanding and relaxing as it passed the information into Chloe's head.

Dylan entered the room wearing the same clothes, but with clean skin and wet hair.

Chloe spoke up proudly; like she was the psychic one, "OK, so you have some message you need to get to people, but you need to gather the people to listen to you? Or something? Right?"

"Yes, that's right. We're on a mission to heal the planet and save people from the dying domes and heal the virus." Mica said matter-of-factly.

Chloe laughed and rolled her eyes.

"Are you crazy! Who do you think you are?"

"You know I can help you with that attitude problem, if you're willing," Mica shot back, wanting to blast Chloe with positive energy.

Dylan spoke up before the girls could argue further "OK, girls, let's just focus here. Yes, we need to gather people to spread the word, but not in a way where we get mobbed; a lot of people will share Chloe's thoughts and think we ARE crazy. We need other people, those who want change, open-minded people."

"Harvard," Nadia blurted out and then shrunk back at her sister's icy stare.

"What?" Mica and Dylan said in unison.

Chloe spoke this time, shutting Nadia up with her eyes. "Our dad is a professor of quantum physics at Harvard. He believes in all this weird stuff. So maybe he can help you. It's a four hour train ride."

"Students! Yes, that's brilliant! They will want change and they'll be open to helping," Dylan thought aloud.

"OK, call your dad then and let him know were coming, maybe he can call a student meeting or something?" Mica thought aloud.

"Fine, I'll be right back but I don't know what I'm going to say, I mean this is all very sudden and a big inconvenience." Chloe said and shot a dirty look to Mica, walking into the kitchen to make the call.

Mica let her thoughts wonder, thinking about what in the heck she was going to say in front of all these Harvard students? She hadn't planned the tree healing in front of the gypsies, it just happened, and surely she wouldn't have that sort of opportunity again. How was she going to get through to people this time? She didn't even heal the tree alone, some unseen force had touched her back and given her more energy to help her. She just hoped that same force would be around the day she told everyone she was going to heal the entire Earth of all its pollutants, because if she couldn't deliver there would be a LOT of angry people.

Then her thoughts drifted to Gran and the boy outside the domes in Sedona. She'd liked her life there; it was a lot less pressure. Even though Gran had known what Mica was doing and had let her go, Mica still missed her terribly and wondered if she should call her. She also thought about the Shiva Lingham and wondered about the possibility of other worlds and if she would ever truly go to one and what would happen. Her grandfather's note had said that her gifts would change; she didn't know what the world would be like if she couldn't see peoples auras or heal their pain. It was weird that all these people were being sought out by some unseen force to help her, wasn't it? Who was giving these psychic people messages to help her?

Dylan broke her chain of thoughts. He whispered softly under his breath, "So are we doing everything right? We go around to all these cities and get as many people as we can to put their hands on the Earth, and in two months time everything will be okay? Right? What if we don't get enough people? And if you're the only one who can heal, how are they going to help?"

Oh no! Mica thought he didn't believe in her, he was questioning why he even came to help her. He grabbed her hand and the shock sparked again, like when he touched her the first time though with less intensity. He pulled away and scrunched his face.

"Sorry, I forgot about that, look I believe in you. I just want to make sure we're doing everything right."

"Do you read my mind or something?" Mica said. Dylan didn't have the large purple third eye like Gretta and Nadia.

Dylan looked alarmed. "No, I just, I dunno, I'm connected to you somehow; I just know what to say sometimes, that's all." Dylan shuffled his feet. The truth was, normally he relied on his crystal to give him information about people, but with her he just knew how she was feeling and what he needed to say.

"I don't know, Dylan." She said, "I was ripped from my home, flown across the world to my dying grandfather's bedside whom I had never met, to be given the task of healing the world. There's no rule book. I'm just going with the flow, OK?" She was nervous, she needed Dylan to be strong, she couldn't do this alone.

"OK," Dylan said smiling. But behind his smile, he felt nervous, nervous about the man at the plane, and about Mica getting hurt. In his dream he had seen her grandfather speak to her, he knew her task was huge, but he knew she could do it, he just didn't want her getting hurt or all hope was lost. All hope for his freedom and for the freedom of all people. He wanted his freedom badly, but it was more than that, he felt a need to protect her from the moment he'd met her. He knew she was fragile inside, and he'd met her to make sure she would be okay.

Chloe entered the room. "OK, I told dad to gather some students for a guest speaker. I told him we were coming with Mica and her dad who worked at NASA and they were going to speak about space' n stuff."

"What? Why didn't you tell him the truth? What's he going to say when you arrive with us?" Mica blurted out.

"Look, how else is my dad going to get students to come out on a Friday night, especially on such short notice to hear someone speak?"

"It's okay, we'll figure it out when we get there. Let's get moving." Dylan was anxious to not stay in one place too long. The memory of last night and Mica telling him that Damian Black had no soul was still very real.

Nadia ran to the fridge and taped up a note for their mother, it said their dad had come to get them after school and taken them for the weekend.

They took the elevator downstairs and walked out onto the curb to hail a cab to the train station. They were a few feet from the cab when Mica screamed, "NO!!!"

Chapter Five
Harvard

Dylan whipped around to see what was wrong and saw Mica staring in a shop window at a small TV screen. On the screen was a picture of her, next to a picture of the late World Leader. Along the bottom it read, "Little girl WANTED for involvement in World Leader Mullen's MURDER! Report sightings to local police." Then the picture changed. It was Damian Black, underneath his picture the caption said, "Damian Black sworn in as New World Leader."

Dylan whispered a cuss word and seized Mica's arm, dragging her limp sobbing body to the taxi with the other girls and Buddha already inside. Tears were falling down her face. Inside the cab, he rifled through his bag to find a baseball cap. He twisted up her hair and stuck it as best he could inside the cap. He would aim for a better disguise later. Mica sat there in shock, lifeless. Buddha jumped out of Nadia's arms and sat on Mica's lap licking her arm.

Everyone thought she had killed the World Leader, who would listen to her now? She thought of the man outside the plane, Damian Black, the one her grandfather warned her about and her skin crawled. He was soulless.

Nadia spoke softly, "Its okay, we all know you didn't do it."

For once Chloe's face softened. "Yeah, and other people will know it too, don't worry."

Mica sucked up her tears and shrank beneath Dylan's cap. They took the cab to the train station and got on the train to Boston. It weaved in and out of the plastic tube, traveling like a snake. They made their way from the New York City dome across a stretch of land that had once probably been a beautiful countryside, but was now black with pollution, and then into the Boston city dome. The space in between the domes was so dark you couldn't see outside; you could only imagine the shriveled trees and black tar streams. Mica imagined people clutching at their throats and fighting for survival. She couldn't believe in forty years people were still alive out there.

She pushed these thoughts out of her mind and decided she needed to tell Dylan about everything, including the Shiva Lingham stone. That it could get them into other worlds when submerged in water but that it would alter their frequency changing their gifts. She pulled him a few seats away from the girls and told him everything; she trusted him with her life. She told him about the prophecy, about the Shiva Lingham, and about Damian Black's plans for the world if they didn't succeed. He listened closely, drinking it all in. Oddly, he wasn't too surprised to hear about other worlds and told her not to tell anyone else about the stone, but to always keep it close to her. She spent the rest of the time on the train thinking about everything her grandfather had told her and what she was going to say to the Harvard students, who thought they were there to hear a NASA rocket scientist speak about space and quantum physics.

Once they arrived in Boston, the sun was just beginning to set. It had been a long day, and Mica and Dylan were tired, and sore from their night of sleeping in the stairwell. Dylan stopped at a drug store and bought some dark make-up to better disguise Mica's fair skin. He gave her his big sweater and with the baseball cap she could almost pass as a little boy. They made their way to Harvard circle, about a twenty-minute walk, and up the giant steps onto Harvard campus. People moved along the stone pathways, students lay in the grass, and some boys were throwing around a football.

They made there way into the science center. Chloe led them down a corridor into an office in the physics department. Sitting behind a dark wooden desk littered with papers and books was a man in his 40's with salt and pepper hair and wire rim glasses. He was bent over some papers, a calculator in one hand and a pen in the other. Mica also noticed a pen behind his ear and one in his mouth; he was chewing on the pen cap when he looked up.

"Daddy!!!" Chloe ran over and jumped on his lap. Nadia walked behind her and gave him a big hug.

"Hey girls, where's your mother and the guest speaker?" he asked, confused and looking around the room. For once Chloe didn't talk; she stepped back, putting Nadia in the limelight. Nadia stood forward and spoke softly and confidently.

"Dad, we came here alone. Mom doesn't know and we lied about the speaker. These are our friends and they're in trouble and need your help. I know how you're always wanting to make a difference in the world, how you wanted to figure out a way to clean the air outside and cure the virus, so we could live freely again. Mica knows how to do that, this is your chance to help. I've seen her heal daddy, she can do this."

Mica watched Nadia's dad as she spoke to him. His aura appeared very accepting of his daughter's words. It shone white, with a lot of lime green, and bright egg yolk yellow, but as Mica looked further she widened her eyes in horror. A huge black blob hovered around his legs, almost as if no energy reached to them, and Mica didn't understand why until he wheeled backwards in his wheelchair. He moved the wheels with his hands and came closer to Nadia.

"You know you have always been special and I believe in your gifts, but, honey, I've been studying for twenty-five years to find a way to release us from the domes, and to cure the virus. I don't think you understand how much damage has been done on the outside. The sun alone would damage us all, not to mention the radiation in the air from all the wars and then there's the virus. We would all parish from the contamination of the ID virus. Not to mention the lack of clean food and water, the list goes on." He looked at Mica and Dylan for the first time.

Mica stepped forward. "I can show you how it can be done. I can reverse global warming and heal everyone who has the virus destroying it forever. Did you call the students for a meeting? I must show as many people as I can and I can't do it alone. When the time comes I will need everyone's energy helping me and believing in me."

"Energy? What do you know about energy? Yes, I called the students, but they think they're coming to hear a lecture from a world-renowned rocket scientist. They think they're coming to learn something." His tone was calm and he wasn't speaking harshly, he was realistic and Mica knew that. She needed to make him understand.

Mica set Buddha down, walked to his desk and grabbed a letter opener that lay across a pile of papers. She then walked over to Dylan and looked him deep in the eyes.

"Do you trust me?" she asked. She could see no other way, everyone wanted proof from her and she had to save the big proof for the crowd of students.

"Yes," he answered, already seeing the wheels turning in her mind, knowing she had his best interest at heart.

She grabbed his arm, barely feeling the now familiar shock every time they touched, and sliced a four-inch gash over the top of it. He bit down in pain but did not cry out. Chloe gasped in horror and their dad wheeled towards Mica in a threatening gesture.

"What's the matter with you? Are you crazy? Son, are you okay?" He asked Dylan.

"Dad, it's OK," Nadia said, watching closely.

When Mica knew he was close enough to see the wound dripping blood she put her hands over Dylan's wet arm. He felt her warmth immediately and a tingling sensation like every severed nerve was calling to each other to reunite. Mica let the bright golden light flow from her fingertips like water, she could feel the blood pulsing and sticking to her hands. Nadia's dad inched closer feeling a change in the air, as he came nearer, the hair on his head stood straight up and he widened his eyes in shock, remarkably resembling Albert Einstein.

"What are you doing to him?" His voice was steadier now and this time he asked the question as a scientist wanting to know the process of what was going on.

Mica breathed, and with it a calmness came over Dylan, nothing hurt any more and he even felt a giddiness in his belly and wanted to laugh. She pulled her hands away and Dylan wiped the blood from his arm, revealing a faint light pink line where the cut used to be.

Their dad wheeled closer in his chair, grabbing Dylan's arm and touching the fresh pink scar.

"Never in all my life did I think I would meet someone who could harness and use the universal life force energy to heal. How did you learn to do that?" Their father asked in absolute astonishment.

"I've known how to heal people all my life. What I didn't know is that I can also heal the air, the trees, even water. I can heal the Earth, I can heal the virus. People have evolved and they can heal too, they just need to believe, they need to believe in themselves and in me. With a mass positive consciousness concentrating on healing the Earth and the contaminated ones, we can change the world."

Their dad smiled. "Well, I'm Dr. Culbertson and I believe in you. I'm not sure if the students are going to believe that this is real when you heal a tiny cut, all the way up on stage where they can't see. They might think it's a joke or a magic trick," he said logically.

"I know," Mica said smiling. "That's why I'm going to heal you." The room was silent.

Mica left Buddha in the office and went down the hall to the bathroom to wash her face but kept the baseball cap on. When she got out, they were all waiting for her. She took a deep breath and they walked down the hallway, each in their own thoughts. You could hear the students piling in, the scraping of chairs, and the sound of notebooks being dropped on the desktops.

Right before he opened the door, Dr. Culbertson pulled Mica aside. "Mica, if you're about to do what I think then I'm very grateful, but it still won't explain how THEY too can heal the Earth when the time comes. I know my students and one of them is going to say that, I want you to be prepared."

Mica hadn't thought of that, she didn't really know how it would work, she had just begun to trust the prophecy and what her grandfather had said.

He spoke again. "So, if you need it, I have a back-up plan." He told her his idea, and she nodded, and he went down the hallway past the door and outside. He returned a few moments later and winked that he was ready.

He opened the door and rolled out onto the stage and all the students, over a thousand of them stood up and clapped. Then Mica grabbed Nadia's arm and told Dylan and Chloe to watch from the front row, she wouldn't need them. Dylan smiled, but Chloe stalked off. Nadia did not question anything. But Mica wanted to be sure this was going to work. She opened the door and stood next to Dr. Culbertson. The clapping stopped.

"Students, I told you that you were going to hear a once in a lifetime lecture and you are. But I lied about who was coming to get you out here on a Friday night." The whole crowd was buzzing and murmuring.

The professor went on, "I know that dome life is all that you have known, that you have grown up fearing the outside world, global warming, the ID virus. But I also know that you would love to travel the open country, the world even, swim in the ocean, feel the heat of the real sun on your face and not the artificial ultra violet ray lights we have. Before the domes were erected in an attempt to save us from what we humans carelessly did to our planet and the spreading ID virus, you could swim with dolphins, jump out of planes, become an astronaut and fly to the moon. Now we sit here and go over old NASA case files and videos and read about old space exploration projects, because it's too dangerous to enter or leave Earth's atmosphere. Wouldn't you like to be free to research parts of the universe in person?" He let the crowd murmur for a moment and than went on.

"Remember my lecture on human energy fields, auras? Although unseen by us they are there and make up who we are, how we function and reflect our state of health. Well, trees, plants, water, and even the Earth has an energy field. Remember the 1998 case I showed you, in which the scientist took an aura photograph of a tree, then cut off its limb and took another photograph revealing the energy of the tree limb still there even after it was severed? Well, the energy of nature is still out there and this little girl can manipulate it in our favor."

He ripped off Mica's hat and everyone gasped and talked loudly, recognizing her as the fugitive on TV. Mica was amazed at Dr. Culbertson's introduction, but she felt nervous because she realized now more than ever that this was a crowd that believed things under one condition: Proof. There would be no faith followers in this building tonight. Mica stepped up to the podium and spoke boldly into the microphone, making sure to use as many big words as possible, trying to sound very intelligent.

"I don't know any scientific words to explain to you how I can heal, but I can repair the world, I can heal the sick. I can see human energy fields, I call them auras, and I can give energy to places in people's auras that have none or are damaged, therefore restoring them back to health." She hesitated, "For example, I can make Dr. Culbertson rise out of his wheel chair and walk to his daughter down in the crowd." She pointed to Chloe and Dylan sitting in front.

Most of the crowd stood, some shifted in they're seats, gasping, not knowing whether she was crazy or not. Some people even shouted out in alarm. Mica felt nervous, because once it had taken her two hours to heal a woman in Sedona from her wheel chair-bound life, working the energy from her head to her toes. Mica didn't know if they would wait that long.

She walked over to Dr. Culbertson and knelt down. She placed her hands on his knees and focused on his aura, she began sending healing energy to his hips and lower back through his knee's and then she would slowly work her way down to his toes, kneading the energy like bread dough working out the kinks. She just hoped they would wait that long.

"I feel light-headed and my hips tingle," he yelled to the crowd. The energy was coming down from the ceiling into Mica's head and out her hands, then into Dr. Culbertson's body. But she knew no one else could see that, so to the crowd it didn't look like she was doing much. After a few minutes of silence someone shouted, "This is a child's game!! This is an unprofessional mockery of science. I'm leaving."

Just then, Mica felt those hands on her back again. So much energy shot out of her hands she flew back three feet and one of the over head lights exploded, sending glass bits and sparks to the ground. Dr. Culbertson shot up out of the wheel chair and picked Mica up off the ground. Spinning her in the air, he said, "I can feel my legs! I can walk! I have been healed." The students gasped in awe. The murmur of their amazement sent a vibration through the room. Dr. Culbertson walked right over to Chloe and hugged her triumphantly. She was smiling and crying at the same time. Then he walked back on stage putting his arm around Mica. After people settled down she spoke again.

"Now you see what can be done, and this same technique can be used on the Earth and its pollutants, giving it that pure life force energy and freeing us from the domes and healing all of the contaminated, wiping out the ID virus. On August 15th, while the sun is rising and the full moon is still visible in the sky, I will do what I just did to Dr. Culbertson, but to the Earth. The healing energy will bathe the trees, the sick water and air but and most of all, it will encompass the contaminated people. We will send a wave of healing energy to all people on Earth."

People were cutting her off, cheering and screaming! Dr. Culbertson spoke now. "But she cannot do it alone. You all must put your hands on the Earth and be grateful for the things Mother Earth has given us and what she can give us if we promise to treat her properly again. You too will be given Mica's gift and can take part in a worldwide miracle. You must go today and convince everyone you know to believe in what we can do.

As scientists, I know this is hard and I'm sure with time and lots of tests on Mica, we could prove that people have evolved. We all know the domes won't last. Nanobots are great for being injected into the human body for a short period of time to repair a kidney, but to become a long-term protective shield, they're not holding up. The Nanobots were an experiment. I'm sure with decades of research someone right here at Harvard could build a better, longer lasting dome, but why? We can be free. Live in a FREEWORLD!" Some people in the crowd were nodding yes, but some had blank stares.

Mica spoke, "I know what you're thinking; how can you do what I can do, it's not possible right? You can't see auras, so you can't help. Right?"

The entire crowd murmured in collective agreement.

"Well, I have set up an experiment to prove that anyone can do what I have done and help us heal the Earth. I need one random person from the crowd." A hundred people shot up from the crowd and Dr. Culbertson pointed to a young man dressed in tan pants and a yellow button down shirt.

"Mark Densy, class President, come up here please." The young man walked proudly to the stage.

Mica grabbed Nadia's hand and led her a few feet from the podium and whispered softly, "I've seen your aura when you trade thoughts with your sister. There is a little white chord going from your head to hers. I need you to tap into my thoughts and my powers and then transfer them into his. Can you do that? It's the only way he can learn to use his own power to think like me, it's what is going to happen August 15th."

"I don't know, I can try," Nadia said nervously.

Dr. Culbertson reached in the side pocket of his wheel chair and pulled out a large glass of muddy water and pulled off the lid. He focused a little camera on it that projected onto a large screen for everyone to see.

"I have gone to the lab and filled this glass of water with polluted liquid," Dr. Culbertson said.

Mica walked up to Mark and led him over to the glass of muddy looking water.

"OK, now hold the palms of your hands a few inches over the glass and focus on your thoughts, don't pull your hands away even if it feels weird," she instructed.

He nodded in agreement. Mica stood about ten feet away with Nadia and started to focus on the water. She could see that the murky water had radioactive particles in it from absorbing the bad pollution from outside the domes. The water's energy was a dark muddy green and so she focused on cleansing it. She looked at Nadia and tuned into her aura; she had a white chord going into Mica's head, but the other chord connecting to Mark was only about five feet away. She wasn't trying hard enough. He wasn't getting her thoughts.

Mica reached out and held Nadia's hand, giving her more energy as well as focusing on the water. The other white chord shot the rest of the five feet into Mark's head. He scrunched his face a little at his thoughts being invaded. Now Mica could see the golden energy flow from his hands to the cup, but it was very faint, not nearly as potent as Mica's.

"I feel heat coming out of my hands," he shouted abruptly. Mica closed her eyes and pushed all of her thoughts about the water to Mark. She appreciated water, loved water and wanted this water healed. He too must appreciate the water and see its negative properties so that he could turn them positive. After two minutes, the crowd started gasping, clapping, screaming. Mica opened her eyes just in time to see the last bit of water turn clear. Mark lowered his shaking hands and turned to the crowd, shock on his face.

"I did it, I healed it. This can be done." The words tumbled out of his mouth like a foreign object.

Just then the side door flew open and twenty secret service men burst onto the stage. In a matter of seconds, they'd grabbed Mica. Mica ripped loose and ran to the podium.

"I didn't kill the World Leader! He was my grandfather; he was poisoned. Just before he died he told me who did it. It was Damian Black, the new World Leader. He made up lies about me to try and stop me from healing the planet. You must believe in everything you saw here today. I will come through on my promise no matter what. Freeworld!"

They seized her and Dr. Culbertson ran forward. "Hey! She is a child. You cannot come in here and take her like this."

A man spoke loudly, "On direct orders from the new World Leader this girl must be brought in for questioning about the late World Leader Mullen's murder." The man's face was stone, void of all emotion.

Dylan jumped up and tackled one of the men nearest Mica. They grabbed Dylan, and he and the man holding Mica ran off stage and into the hallway.

"Buddha!!!" Mica was screaming. "Buddha!!!" She repeated in desperation.

Mica wore the purple bag with the Shiva Lingham in it around her shoulder the whole time, and she would leave her crystals' case and duffle bag but she could not leave without Buddha. Buddha came running down the hall from Dr. Culbertson's office where he was staying. Mica flailed her arms and squirmed out of the man's grip just in time to grab Buddha before the man grabbed Mica by her long hair.

"Owwww!" Mica let out a gasp.

"Hey, child abuse!! You will go to jail for that, don't touch her like that," Dylan screamed.

With one hand, the man smacked Dylan hard across the face. Once outside, a black helicopter was waiting for them. Mica had never in all of her life harmed another person, but she saw no other way. She wondered that if she could give energy to someone's body and aura, then maybe she could also take it away, causing harm. She focused on the man holding her in his grip. He was bad, very angry, he had large red blobs woven with black into his aura. She focused on his heart chakra, a three-inch muddy green blob in his chest, and for the first time ever Mica pulled the energy to her and not from her. She felt his darkness and hate coming into her hands and wanted to stop but knew she must go on if she wanted to be free. The man clutched his chest and broke a sweat.

"Ahhh, my chest, I can't breathe, arghh." He let go of her in an instant. She ran over to Dylan and came up behind the man that had a hold of him and she took her sack with the heavy Shiva Lingham stone and whacked him on the head. The man let out a cry and released Dylan, clutching his head. The men in the helicopter looked alarmed and started running out. Just then the door burst open and the rest of the secret service men approached the grass. The man lying on the lawn stopped clutching his chest and regained strength. Mica saw no other way. There was a large fountain just twenty feet from them.

"Dylan we must use the stone."

He looked at her, raising his eyebrows, and they both started running. Mica handed a barking Buddha to Dylan and pulled out the Shiva Lingham as they ran. In one hand Mica held the Shiva Lingham, and with her other she held Dylan's. Her mind was racing. Where would they end up? With what powers? Would they ever be able to come back? What did her grandfather's letter say about concentrating on a world that had certain things? She didn't care, the men were ten feet from them and she heard bullets snapping into the grass at her feet. These damn guns were supposed to be outlawed! She thought. Then with one giant leap for salvation she plunged into the fountain, trailing Dylan and Buddha behind her, and with her left hand out she submerged the Shiva Lingham in water, thinking, "A safe world, a safe world."

In an instant, her vision went blank and she felt every cell of her body tingle, making her nauseous. She felt like she was being pulled on a roller coaster without tracks. Just floating aimlessly through the sky. Then her backside made hard contact with the ground.

Chapter Six
New World

Faintly she felt Dylan's hand; she opened her eyes and looked around. They were in jail! Oh, no, it didn't work. She had blacked out when she hit the fountain and the men took her to jail!

"Your hair! Your eyes!" Dylan cried out. Mica looked at Dylan, his eyes were amber brown and he had one royal blue streak in his hair right in front.

"Are we in another world?" Mica asked dreamily.
She tried to focus on Dylan's aura and couldn't. She couldn't see his aura!

"I can't see your aura, we must be, my powers have changed. What color is my hair? Yours is blue."

"Yours is blue too! Maybe in this world everyone has blue streaks in their hair." Dylan offered. Buddha barked from under Dylan's coat and pranced out with a little orange-colored chunk in his hair. Mica and Dylan laughed.

"I guess everyone's hair is colored here. How do we get out of here? If we alert someone that we're here, they might freak out as to how we got in here right?"

Buddha, sitting next to Dylan started growling looking over Mica's shoulder. Mica was facing Dylan, so whatever Buddha was growling at was behind her back.

"Buddha, what is it?" Mica turned around for the first time in the jail cell. What she saw stole her breath; she closed her eyes tight and opened them again. Her grandpa, and two people that must be her mother and father were all standing in the cell right behind Mica. They were murky and see-through, they were ghosts. Mica's mother wore a white sundress and she smiled at Mica and waved. Her hair was white like Mica's and her fair skin glowed. Her grandfather blew her a kiss and her dad gripped his heart, beaming at her.

"What is it?" Dylan asked, alarmed by Mica staring off in the distance.

"I think I know what my power in this world is. I see ghosts." The words felt bizarre after leaving her lips, but they were true. The hair on Dylan's arms prickled.

"Right now? You're seeing ghosts right now? I don't see anything." Dylan squinted to be sure.

"My family is standing right there." Mica pointed to the brick wall. "I don't think they can speak to me. Do you think they have been with me since they died?"

Mica's mother nodded no.

"Oh, they said no. Well are you with me because I'm in danger?"

Mica's mothers face lit up; she nodded yes and reached out to touch Mica's chin. Mica stood still in anticipation, but didn't feel a thing as the murky hand passed through her face. Mica's grandfather took two of his fingers and tapped on his temple.

"What, my head?" Mica asked confused.

"What's going on? What is my power?" Dylan was wondering out loud.

"My grandpa is telling me to use my head," Mica said, arching her eyebrows in confusion.

Just then Mica heard a deep voice inside her head. *"Your mind, use your mind."* Mica jolted upright.

"Oh great, Dylan, I'm hearing voices in my head." This was all too weird.

"What do you mean? Are they talking to you?"

"Make him focus to find his power; you must get out of here." Her grandfather tapped his temple again. The three of them stood there patiently, and Mica told Dylan what they said.

"Okay, so close your eyes and focus your mind. Like meditating," Mica encouraged.

"I don't meditate," Dylan said, frustrated that the pressure was on him.

Dylan closed his eyes, but he didn't know what to concentrate on. In the domed world, he knew to focus on the voice of his crystal, but here it was different. His crystal wouldn't talk. His frequency had changed, so he needed to change his focus to his new undiscovered power. He breathed deeply and with the out breath, he began to feel very small. Mica gasped and he opened his eyes.

She was huge! The room was gigantic, Buddha growled at him and went to put him in his mouth. Mica reached out, stopping Buddha.

"You're so tiny!" Mica screamed.

"What happened, how tall am I?"

"Maybe a foot, probably ten inches." Mica couldn't help it, she was trying to hold it in, but she busted out laughing. Seeing him so small was different. Dylan turned bright red and inhaled deeply, becoming large size again.

"Don't laugh at me! You're hearing voices and seeing dead people, and we're stuck in jail in another world, I hardly think this is funny! Typical American, laughing when it's inappropriate." Mica stopped her laughing immediately, even though his British accent made it even funnier but she held her tongue. Mica slipped the Shiva Lingham back into her purple velvet bag.

"Ok, I'm sorry. Can you become small again, so you can slide through the bars and maybe find a key to get us out of here?" Mica asked in her sweetest voice.

"Fine!" Dylan breathed out and felt himself shrink and the world grow. He walked through the bars and down the hallway, hearing a TV blaring loudly. He followed the sound and came to a little alcove down the hall where there was a very large man snoring loudly in his seat. He was wearing a green police uniform and he had a yellow streak in his hair. Dylan saw keys lying on the desk, but he was too small to reach them.

He breathed in deeply, concentrating on being big but only big enough to reach the keys and not wake the man. He was maybe four feet tall now and quietly grabbed the keys off the desk. He started walking away, when he heard the snoring stop. He panicked and made himself really small, about three inches tall, but the keys were too big for him to hold now so they clanked to the floor and the man grunted and opened his eyes. Dylan ran up against the wall watching the man. He looked around and then his eyelids slowly started closing again. Dylan made himself a bit bigger and grabbed the keys and walked back down toward the cell, but before rounding the corner he became full size. He walked up to the cell and clicked it open with the key.

"Is there anyone out there?" Mica asked, slipping Buddha into her purple bag.

"Just one guard and he's sleeping."

Mica followed Dylan as they tiptoed down the hall. All the other jail cells were empty. Once they got near the alcove, they heard the snoring and proceeded to walk past the desk. Dylan walked up to lay the keys down, where they had been, and the phone rang. The guard jumped up and on seeing Dylan and Mica standing right there, he flew back a few feet. He picked up the phone and slammed it back down.

"What are you kids doing in here?" he asked groggily.

Dylan stood there frozen.

Mica spoke sweetly, "Our dad didn't come home last night, we were wondering if he might be here? He drinks a lot."

"Ain't no one here today." The man was confused.

"Oh, okay, he's probably sleeping it off. Thank you" Mica grabbed Dylan's arm and ran out the front door.

"Stupid kids." The guard breathed.

Once outside the police station, Mica had a wild thought. She looked up and saw the big beautiful sky.

"Dylan there are no domes, we're in a free world!"

Dylan looked around wildly. There were green trees littering the street and small colorful flowers in front of the shops. This world looked the same as home, but it didn't have domes and looked a bit older and healthier and more colorful. The roads were brick and the shops were quaint.

Mica's grandpa appeared and spoke to her mind. *"All worlds overlay exactly. So if you were to go back home, you would still be in Boston where it's unsafe, you must make your way west a couple hundred miles and then go back and finish your task."*

Mica told Dylan and he agreed to move west. Mica started thinking about the possibility of getting a car. *"You must take the train."* her mother interjected. Mica looked over and saw her mother smiling at her. It was weird to see her like this. She had never met her, never knew her, and here she was in spirit, trying to help Mica on this quest. At that thought, Mica got a flash of images from her mother about how much she had loved her. The day she was born and her mother holding her in the hospital, kissing her face and her father rocking her in his arms, and Mica's mother wearing the pink rose quartz necklace. Mica let a tear fall down her face and then pushed the thoughts aside and spoke to Dylan.

"We should take the train, do we have money here?"

"Barely. I spent the last bit on hotdogs in Central Park and that dark make-up, but maybe we can sneak onboard."

They passed a bookshop, and Mica noticed that a few stores up there were dozens of spirits crowding in a shop, spilling out the front door.

"Umm, let's cross the street," Mica offered, trying to avoid walking past all of the ghosts. She went to cross and her dad was standing in front of her. *"You must go in that shop and help, they will give you money."* Mica realized her dad had a British accent like Dylan's. She loved seeing her parents, but was already getting annoyed with their constant interference.

"Wait," she told Dylan. "We're supposed to go in that shop." She pointed and read for the first time the sign hanging over the building. "Psychic twenty-four hours."

"Oh great, another psychic," Dylan said.

Mica sighed.

"Well let's get this over with."

She got closer to the building and noticed all of the spirits staring at her. She made her way through them, feeling a chill in her bones. Inside was a waiting room with a few rows of chairs against the wall filled with people. Past them was a green and gold-striped curtain. Mica walked back and hollered beyond the curtain.

"Hello."

The curtain flew back and a middle-aged Asian woman with black silk hair and a white streak stared at Mica.

"Can I help you little girl, I'm busy?"

There was the spirit of an older Asian lady with black hair standing behind her waving feverishly at Mica. She had a necklace in her hand and was pushing it in Mica's face. *"Tell her I left her my necklace in-between the mattresses of my bed."* The woman spoke into Mica's mind. *"I'm her mother and she's been looking for it."*

"Your deceased mother wants me to tell you she left you that necklace in-between the mattresses of her bed."

The woman's jaw dropped open. "You see spirits? You can really see them!" Now the people behind Mica in the waiting room were standing up. They were whispering, "She talks to spirits, she really can see them."

Dylan stepped up on a chair and turned around. "Yes, she talks to spirits, and for twenty dollars each, she will give you messages from loved ones from the other side!"

Everyone started rustling through their purses. Mica looked at Dylan, shocked at his brilliance. They could make money for the trip west! Mica whispered to the Asian shop owner.

"Let me use your shop for a bit and I'll give you five bucks a person."

"Deal," the woman said and opened the curtain, ushering Mica inside. "I'm Jezebel. There's something special about you, you aren't from around here are you?" Mica just smiled and looked around the room. There was a card table with a black cloth on it and two chairs. A woman who sat in one of the chairs got up as Mica entered. Two white candles flickered on the table, giving the room a golden glow. Mica sat in one chair and Jezebel left through the curtain to wait for her money.

Dylan and Buddha took the money from the people and sent them in. Each person had a ghost of a family member or friend there with something to say. For over two hours Mica gave these people their messages until the last person was gone. After giving Jezebel her cut, Dylan and Mica had made $300 dollars. Just before leaving the store, Dylan stopped Mica. "So, umm, are there any more spirits around? Like anyone around me?" he asked nervously.

Mica realized he must have been wondering why his parents hadn't come to see him as hers had.

"No, Dylan that's it, I'm sorry."

"Whatever, I don't care. Let's go." He stalked off hiding his face.

She and Buddha followed him. She too wondered why his parents hadn't come. She wondered if Dylan looked like his dad. It was already dark out and using the directions Jezebel had given them they walked in silence to the train station. When they turned the block to the train Dylan stopped. "You go up and buy one ticket, I'm going to make myself small and hide in your bag to save us money, we're going to need it."

"Wait, isn't that dishonest?" Mica added.

Dylan rolled his eyes and became small, dismissing her question. She picked him up and scooped him into her front sweater pocket. Buddha growled in confusion. As she approached the platform, looking around for the ticket counter, a guard stared at her and spoke into his walkie-talkie. Mica gulped air nervously, wondering if they were also in trouble in this world for something. She approached the ticket counter.

"One ticket west please."

"How far west, you can't just say west." The stubbly man had a muddy brown streak in his fair blonde hair and he glared at her.

"Well, I can't remember the name of the state, its got a big desert and...."

"Azonia?"

"Yes, Azonia! That's it, one ticket there, please." Mica hoped it was the same as Arizona in her world. The man looked to the guard.

"Shouldn't you be in school?" he asked, raising his eyebrows, eyeing her and the guard in the distance.

"Oh, yes, I should be. I can't wait to get back to Azonia with all of my school friends! My parents are waiting for me." The teller's face shot up glaring her in the eye.

"Liar!" he screamed. The guard was now jogging over and Mica was panicking. She could feel Dylan jiggling in her pocket.

"I'm not lying! You better give me my ticket or my parents will sue you!" Mica fired back in fear. The guard was now at the window.

"What's the problem?" he asked the ticket man.

"This girl was just lying to me, she said she is waiting to get back to her parents in Azonia. Clearly she has no parents, I think she fled Berkshire Prep."

The guard looked at her, "You all alone here? Did you really say you were waiting to get back to your PARENTS?" The guard hounded her, amplifying the word parents.

"My Aunt Jezebel just dropped me off, and yes I am waiting to get back to Azonia with my parents and go back to school" Mica said confidently.

The guard seized her at once.

"You lie, orphan! You're a blue, blues don't got parents, and you know it! Back to Berkshire Preparatory orphanage!"

He dragged Mica away from the counter, kicking and screaming. Buddha barked wildly and Dylan was frantically deciding whether or not to make himself big enough to fight the guard. He decided to keep out of sight. The guard threw Mica into the back of a golf cart that had been turned into a police car. They rode down the street with the wind in Mica's hair. She clung to her bag that had the Shiva Lingham rock in it. Buddha was perched just on top of the rock with his head peeking out. It's like he was protecting it. Mica put her finger in her pocket to let Dylan know she didn't forget him and she tried not to crush him with her bag.

After a five-minute ride, they turned down a long cobblestone road and came upon a stone sign, which said, "Berkshire Preparatory Orphanage," and under that in smaller letters, "Classing up society's motherless youth." Mica felt a lump in her throat. Motherless youth? Ouch, this place sounded awful. She decided that when she met the principal of this school she would ask to wash her hands and then in the bathroom she would submerge the Shiva Lingham and get them out of here and into another world where they could make it farther west.

The school looked like a large 18th century jail. Ivy vines crept up the crumbling brick walls. They approached the circular driveway and a stubby woman walked up to them, her lips were pursed so that you were not sure if she was smiling or frowning. Both hands were in her apron pockets which she wore over a navy ankle-length skirt. She raised her eyes at Buddha and nodded to the policemen, the red streak in her hair screamed evil especially in comparison to her dark sleek black bob.

"Oh, yes, she is one of ours, thank you Officer Dubiel." She raised one eyebrow beckoning Mica out of the cart. As Mica made her way to the curb to stand beside the woman, the policeman tipped his hat at the evil woman and drove off. The woman grabbed Buddha and ripped him out of Mica's bag. Mica screamed and the woman threw her hand over Mica's mouth.

"No dogs allowed!"

A smaller, but just as evil-looking, woman approached out of the front doors and took Buddha, walking away from the building and out into the wooded area. Mica's mother came out of nowhere and started following the woman into the woods after Buddha. Mica wondered if she could do anything.

"No wait! I don't go here and that's MY dog, let him go. Buddha!!!" Mica's throat was raw.

"I'll be taking your purse as well. There's someone in the office who wishes to see you."

With that, she ripped the purple velvet bag off of Mica's shoulder and grabbed her underarm, leading her inside. Dylan heard everything and wondered who was waiting to see Mica? Jezebel is the only person they know in this world!

Once they turned the corner, Mica froze. Her grandfather materialized out of nowhere, shaking his fist at Damian Black who stood in the Dean's office cowering at Mica from behind a desk. He was dressed in a long black trench coat with the collar flipped up around his neck. Then it dawned on Mica that she was in another world, so everyone must have their twin and this man wasn't the same one she knew who'd killed her grandfather, the one without a soul, was he?

"My little Mica, so nice to see you. Buddha will be taken to the animal pound and put to sleep. Put to sleep forever," he said with a grin. Okay, I guess he is the same man, she thought.

"Also we are keeping your special rock safe, oh, yes, I know what it does, I have a similar one." He pulled out a necklace with a small Shiva Lingham hanging from it. It was the size of a grape, not even a tenth of the size of Mica's.

"It can't be that powerful seeing as though its sooooo TINY, I'm surprised you made it here in one piece. CON-GRAT-U-LATIONS" she said drawling out the last part and giving him her iciest stare.

The soulless man grabbed Mica's hair and pulled her close to him. Then he bore into her eyes.

"I'm going to keep you here for the next two months just to be sure that everyone back in our world knows you're a fake, psychotic, lying, murderer!"

Dylan couldn't take it anymore. He rose up out of her pocket, ripping the stitches as he grew. He was so angry and put so much force into his growth that he wasn't sure how big he'd grown until his head bumped into the ceiling. It seemed that as well as shrinking he could also grow as large as a giant! Damian Black let go of Mica and jumped back wide-eyed.

"There you are, my dear boy." The words were barely out of Damian's mouth before Dylan's arms were around his neck choking out the air left in that last word. Damian's arms shot up, but they were no match for the twelve-foot tall boy. He glared into Dylan's eyes, penetrating his very essence. Dylan stared back into those seemingly endless black pits until they became like windows and for a second he thought he saw his mother screaming. He blinked, loosening his grip, and focusing his eyes to see better. But that was the opportunity Damian Black needed to duck and plunge his hands into his shirt and put the small Shiva Lingham in his mouth, wetting it, and in a matter of seconds he was gone.

There was a commotion down the hallway, and Mica's grandfather, still in the room spoke into Mica's mind. *"Dylan must be small again, let them take you into the school or you will never find Buddha again. You will never make it out of this world. Do not fight."* Dylan was already halfway out the door when Mica stopped him.

"No Dylan! You have to hide in my pocket again or we will never get home!" Mica pleaded.

"But I can take them, look at me, I'm huge." Dylan was geared up and a bit too cocky about his new size.

The noises were getting closer. "Please Dylan! Trust me." He shrank at once and Mica scooped him into her pocket just as three guards and the evil woman came rushing in.

"What's all this noise? Where's Mr. Black? What have you done, child?" The woman hissed through barely clenched teeth.

"Oh, he had an appointment." Mica smiled nonchalantly. The woman looked around the room, seeing signs of a struggle and smirked.

"Lock her in the dormitories," she spat at her guards.

They forcibly walked Mica down the hallway, their loud boots clicking on the wood floors. They reached a giant set of double doors and the guard pulled out a key ring, unlocked the door, throwing her inside and slamming it shut. Mica hit the ground with such force the breath was knocked out of her. She recovered and looked around. A dozen small girls dressed in rags were peering up at her from their bunks. One of them, a tall girl about fifteen years old, with red wiry hair and a bright blue streak in front jumped up, she was clearly the leader of the pack.

"Who are you? Where did you come from?" she asked in a weary tone.

"I'm Mica from Azonia," she said with a shaky voice.
Mica peered around and noticed all the girls in the room had the same blue streak in their hair.

"So what do the colored streaks in the hair mean?" Mica asked them unable to contain her curiosity any longer. The red headed leader frowned at Mica's question.

"How is it that you don't know that, you're from Azonia not another world." She laughed at this. Mica tensed up.

"Oh, well, my last orphanage beat me every time I asked a question so I don't know much, then that evil woman took my doggie." Mica was tearing up now, because she missed Buddha, but it helped the girls to believe her story. All the girls gathered round. "Awe you poor thing," one of them said.

"All the blues are orphans and live here learning how to sew, cook, read, write, and work in the fields. Then at eighteen, we are sold as nannies and maids and our hair turns white until we get married or take another job, if we ever get married. You must know that the colored streak in everyone's hair is there soul. Reds are aggressive and yellows are loyal and so on." The red-head said.

"Oh, yeah, duh! I know that," Mica said, but obviously she'd lied and was fascinated by it all, it was kind of like an aura except they wore it for everyone to see.

The red-head spoke again, "And that evil woman that you speak of is Lady Marcelle and we all hate her. If you call her Miss Marcelle or Lady Marcy she will beat you to a pulp with her rod." All the children winced, surely they had all been beaten. Mica's tears were starting up again at the thought of these poor girls living here.

Then a huge bang came from nowhere and only Mica jumped. Over a loud speaker, the evil woman said, "Lights out, go to bed…NOW!"

The girls hurried to their cots, the red-head looked back at Mica, "She will check on us in two minutes; we must be asleep."

Mica looked around for a bed and saw none open, then someone threw a pillow at her and a sheet. She ran to the end of the line of bunks and threw her pillow down; lay on the cold concrete (careful not to crush Dylan) and threw the sheet over herself, just in time for the big double doors to open. She closed her eyes. She heard clip clop, clip clop coming closer, until she knew the evil woman was hovering over her. For thirty seconds, Mica didn't breathe, then the noise receded and the doors shut again. The entire room drew a collective sigh of relief, but they dared not speak a word, and then they fell asleep for real. Mica didn't even want to know what happened if you were caught not sleeping or going to the bathroom when Lady Evil was walking in. Mica lay there wondering how she was going to get out of this and wondering when she had last eaten, it must have been hours ago in Central Park. Meeting Nadia and Chloe and speaking at Harvard seemed like days ago. Everything was happening so fast.

She took Dylan out of her pocket and took off her shoes. She folded her sock in half and lay him inside her shoe. Dylan was upset that he had to stay small for so long but there seemed no other way. A terror ran through him at the thought that if he slept in his small size and woke up, would he be small forever? He shut out the thought and went to sleep in Mica's shoe, which actually didn't smell too badly, maybe because his nose was so tiny. Then Dylan and Mica fell off to a long awaited sleep with empty tummies and a surprise the next morning.

Chapter Seven
Lady Evil

She awoke to the sounds of barking. Mica squinted her eyes; the other girls were running around frantically.

"Who's got candy, or a pet they shouldn't, she's coming with those beasts and when she finds it, we will ALL be beaten!!!" The red-headed leader said. The barking was getting louder now, and she flew across the room at top speed into Mica's face. "What are you hiding? We're all going to get beaten!"

Mica was blank for a second, then Dylan walked out of her shoe and grew big; every girl in the place gasped and a few of them even fainted or started praying.

"It's me they're looking for, I can become real small to hide. It's a power I have. Help hide me and I will help you with anything!" Dylan said urgently.

Mica didn't even have time to intervene, the red-head recovered quickly and ran with Dylan to the edge of the room. She stood on a stool and said, "Be small! NOW!"

Dylan obeyed and she scooped him up, removing the metal grate, and put him in the air conditioning vent. "Hopefully, he won't freeze," she mumbled.

She had just put the stool away when the doors burst open and Lady Evil, as Mica now liked to refer to her, walked over to Mica and whispered, "I spoke to Mr. Black and he says we can keep you forever, we just need to find the boy."

"Release the wolves!" she shouted.

Wolves, Mica thought, I thought they were dogs. All the girls jumped up on their beds, to avoid being attacked, and the wolves ransacked the entire room, ready to rip someone's throat out at the slightest movement, at least that's how everyone felt. They were grayish white, their fur matted down so you could see the girth of their giant bodies, their teeth were huge and stained reddish from their last meal. The wolves sniffed around, until they all came to the spot right below the air vent. Mica tensed. The girls were pros at this and they all looked absolutely indifferent. Lady Evil walked over to the place where the wolves were and looked up. Mica couldn't breathe.

"Bring me a chair," she shouted. She got up on the chair and opened the shaft to the air vent. Then she picked up a wolf by the scruff of its neck and threw it in the shaft. It ran down the tunnel, barking madly, it's claws clicking on the metal.

That's when Mica lost it. "Please no! Don't kill him he's a human being!!!"

Lady Evil pursed her lips at the submission, she stepped off the chair and reached behind her back, brandishing a small wooden stick with two wires running up the side. Every girl in the room drew in a breath for they knew what was about to happen. Mica winced, wishing Dylan or her grandfather would appear out of nowhere to save her from the pain she knew was about to be inflicted upon her.

The woman flipped Mica onto her stomach on the bunk and raised the weapon. It came down onto Mica's back, but not just a hard slap of wood, it jolted her every muscle. Before Mica's brain could figure out what was different about this feeling, the woman had beaten her again and again until Mica realized she was being beaten and electrocuted! The wires on the side gave the weapon electricity, and every time it hit Mica's skin, it jolted her teeth. In her mind, she vowed right then and there to get every girl out of this horrid place. She felt like a cattle being prodded into action. She took her beating, crying out when it was too much. When she thought she could take no more, the wolf came back through the air vent. The wolf came back without Dylan. The faintest smile touched Mica's lips before she collapsed. He was alive.

"No studies today, you're locked in this room without meals until the boy resurfaces. Hide him and you won't live to regret it." Her eyes scanned the girls, burning her words into their minds.

After the wolves were gone and Lady Evil had left, Mica moved in and out of consciousness. The girls lay wet washcloths on her back and gave her water. After a few hours, she came around fully.

"I feel like I'm dying, it hurts so much. Does she always do that for punishment?" Mica asked shakily.

This time, a little underweight girl, with mousy brown hair and a pale blue streak, answered, "Not usually that bad, she got you good. She doesn't always turn on the electricity. I could hear it buzzing from over here." The little girl had tears in her eyes as she slipped her hand into Mica's.

It was hours before Dylan came back. He was bursting to talk with Mica, but wasn't sure if he should make himself known in the room. He had been crouching in the air vent for thirty minutes now and had decided it was safe. He made himself big enough to remove the grate and peeked his head out. The girls were all crouched around a bed.

"Mica," he whispered.

The girls turned, and one of them got a stool to help Dylan down. He made himself normal size and walked to the bed, the alarm showing on his face at seeing the state Mica was in. She was paler than usual and sweating with pain.

"That monster, what did she do?" he screamed.

She opened her eyes, gazing up at him. "Your OK! I was so worried. Don't worry about me, I'm fine," She tried to sit up and winced in pain. Dylan's face flared red in anger at who had done this to her.

"Mica, there's boys here too, I've been to their dorms. They are treated horribly, like slaves. We need to get them out of here, this is no place to live." Before Mica could reply, a few of the girls started desperately asking about some of the boys, wondering if their brothers were okay. Dylan couldn't reassure them, because he didn't know many of their names. Mica smiled, realizing that Dylan was a mirrored reflection of her soul in male form. "I want to get the girls out too, we must escape."

"Escape!" The red-head blurted out. "Are you crazy! Even if we could get out of here, Lady Marcelle would catch us in no time and beat us beyond recognition." The girls shrank behind her at the thought of a beating.

Mica made a quick decision to trust these girls. She saw no other way, they would find out sooner or later. "Dylan and I aren't from around here," she said, letting the words linger only a moment and then added, "like not from this world." The collective intake of breath was unmistakable; they wanted to believe her, but didn't know how they could wrap their minds around what she was saying.

"Dylan has powers, like you saw, and so do I. We are going to get you all out of here and take you back to our world, where orphans are treated with respect. They go to families; they are told 'I love you' everyday, and they can play in the yard, paint, play sports or just sit around all day watching movies. Being an orphan doesn't mean there's anything wrong with you and people in our world will take you in and you can have a better life and no one, I mean absolutely no one, gets beaten, whipped, or hit." All the girls were mumbling now in excited tones. The red-head stepped forward. "If you're lying, I mean you can't tell us this and get our hopes up and not come through. Can you really get us out of here? Forever?" Out of the corner of the room Mica's mother and father walked in and smiled.

"Yes," Mica said. With that they started in on the plan. Mica's mother knew where Buddha was hidden, in a shed on the grounds, just a short walk into the woods where the gardener lived. Her father had followed Lady Evil when she'd hidden the Shiva Lingham under her own bed inside her sleeping quarters. He went back later and confirmed that she is guarding her door with one of those wolves.

So Mica sent Dylan off to get Buddha, and by then it would be lights out and the rest of the plan could go into effect. While Dylan was gone, Mica got all of the girls up to speed and told them about the Shiva Lingham stone. She really wished she didn't have to tell so many people, but she saw no other way. They were going to see it very very soon, and more importantly, they were going to experience first-hand what it did.

They were all starving, but they'd just have to wait until they returned to her world to eat. It dawned on Mica that she didn't know any of the girls' names and they hadn't asked hers. She thought maybe it was because they had no individuality here and no need for a name. They were slave orphans with no future. Mica felt increasingly better about getting them out of here. Just as they were finishing the plan, the big double doors opened and everyone froze in their place.

"It's me," Dylan said.

Mica knew he would be coming through that door if he'd gotten the key, but it was still scary. Buddha knew to be silent, but he leapt out of Dylan's arms and onto Mica's lap as she was still propped up in bed. Mica didn't want to alarm anyone, but she wasn't sure if when the time came she would be able to walk. She had never been beaten or electrocuted in her life, so this was all new to her. Just as Buddha jumped up, Mica winced, and he sensed her pain whining as she stroked his fur. "I'm okay, baby boy, I love you, and I won't let anyone take you away from me ever again." Buddha whimpered a sad thank you.

Dylan made himself small and crept through the vents to the boys' sleeping quarters and caught the boys up on the plan and went back to be with Mica.

After climbing out of the vent, he sat on the edge of her bed.

"Can I speak to Mica alone, girls?" They smiled as they left, so happy to oblige to anything because they were getting out of here.

Mica sensed Dylan's worries, he was the worrier she was the dreamer.

He began, "OK, so, you have to remember we are still in Boston. When we go back to our world we could be inside the Harvard library for all we know. People will be looking for you and so once we appear in that world, we need to re-wet the Shiva Lingham and go anywhere. The girls and boys will be safe."

"I know, I know, I don't want to linger either. I'm excited to leave this place. My powers kind of suck here. I miss seeing auras." They both laughed at that. Mica winced at the pain it took for her to laugh, her whole body ached.

"One day, I'll come back here and," Dylan started but Mica knew what he was going to say and she put two fingers over his lips. "No, you're not going to come back here and hurt Lady Evil, Karma will take care of her." He grabbed her hand from his lips and brought it back down to her lap.

"You're so nice, Mica, so forgiving. I wish I could be like that."

She looked into his eyes; he was being sincere, "Oh, thanks," Mica said nervously. Her face was red now and she looked at Dylan. He stared back at her with an unwavering strength, she leaned a little closer and looked right into his eyes, just as the redhead rounded the corner. "It's time! We need to get going with the plan."

Mica jolted upright. "OK, let's go," she blurted out.

Dylan stood up blushing. "Alright, let's do this," so the plan began.

All of the girls huddled in the long bathroom amongst the rows of sinks. One sink in particular was full of water. Dylan was to unlock the boys door so they could make their way to Mica and the girls dorm. Then he was to head over to Lady Evil's sleeping quarters. Before Dylan left, Mica had a long conversation with her father, taking complete directions of where Dylan was to go. As she was talking to him, she realized she wouldn't be able to see them again after she left this world.

Mica sat in bed alone now thinking. Just as she thought about them her mother, father and grandfather appeared. Mica looked around, sad now to say goodbye, but knowing that was why they had come back.

"I will miss you all, thank you for your help. I'm sorry we never really got to just hang out." Her eyes were welling up with tears now.

Her mother spoke softly inside her head, *"I will always be with you when you need me, I'll be the wind in your hair, a tug at your heart. I'm so proud of you and all of the things you will do."* Then she disappeared.

"I'm so grateful you came to a world where your gift was seeing us, I want you to know whenever you are in trouble, I will be there fighting right beside you. I love you little one," and with that her father was gone. Lastly, her grandfather stood before her. Mica was freely crying now. *"You know those hands you felt on your back when you needed more energy to heal the tree and the water?"* Mica sat up further and Buddha tumbled off her lap.

"That was me, and I will not leave you until you have fulfilled your task." He smiled, gazing at her.

"Can I do it? Can I really save the people from the domes, and heal the planet and the virus?" she asked.

"You have the ability, but you must believe in yourself. So many forces are working in your favor, dear child. Just know that the universe bends to your will, because your will is pure." Mica started to think that over, and just then the two doors opened and fifteen little scruffy-haired boys crept in and her grandfather was gone.

Dylan had unlocked the boys door and set them free. He'd then gone to the kitchen to steal a big hunk of meat for the wolf, and now walked down the corridor to Lady Evil's bedroom as the boys made their way to the girl's dorm. His heart was pounding, it wasn't very late, maybe eleven o'clock. What if she was still awake? What if she slept with the Shiva Lingham under her pillow? Dylan didn't like violence, but for what she'd done to Mica, he would gladly unleash a load of anger on this woman and if it came to it, he was willing to hurt her. He knew Mica wouldn't want him to but he almost welcomed a confrontation.

As he came around the corner, he saw the massive beast lying in front of her big double doors, erect and ready to pounce. At the sight of Dylan, the wolf whipped his head around in one swift movement and got up on his rear hind legs, letting out a deep snarl. Dylan froze for a moment under that gaze and then threw the meat a few feet away from the door. The wolf merely looked at it, his nostrils flaring. He looked as if he wanted to eat Dylan, not some small hunk of meat. His growling grew louder, and Dylan knew he couldn't run; that would trigger the animals' instinct to chase and this thing would be on his back tearing out precious flesh in a moment. He did the only thing he could think of and took a deep breath, growing to the height of the 12-foot ceiling. Dylan let out a growl of his own.

At the sight of his growth, the wolf cast down his eyes and tucked his tail between his legs, grabbing the meat before he ran off down the hall. Dylan slowly opened the door, peering in the room. Lady Evil was balled up in bed snoring, with an eye mask on, he shrank down to a few inches and slipped through the crack in the door. His little feet could not carry him fast enough across the long room, so again he grew a little bigger, about a foot tall, but as he reached the bed a voice boomed behind him.

"I've been waiting for you," Dylan froze, reducing himself to an inch tall at the sound of Damian Black's voice. He ran under the bed and quickly found the Shiva Lingham, which looked like a mountain in his small size.

He heard movement and a woman's voice. He grew large enough to roll the rock out and as soon as he was out from underneath the bed he raised to his biggest size ever. He ballooned with strength to over fifteen feet tall, ducking his head at the ceiling; the rock was tiny in his hands. Damian Black was at his feet and Lady Evil shrieked in surprise, but regained herself quickly. Dylan was still stunned at what had happened earlier, when he'd looked in

Black's eyes back in Lady Evils office and he made a mental note not to do it again. Just as he walked for the door, he felt a whip at his back and a shock ran through his body. He lost his concentration and became normal size dropping the Shiva Lingham. Damian cackled with laughter.

Black picked him up by the shirt collar, and Dylan closed his eyes not wanting to hear his mother scream. The bookcase behind Black started shaking and Dylan sprang his eyes open just in time to see every book flying off the shelf, smacking Black and Lady Evil in the head. Dylan sat there dumbfounded for a moment and then felt a little push at his back. His crystal spoke, *Mica's parents are helping you, RUN*!

Dylan grabbed the Shiva Lingham and leaped out of the way just as the ceiling fan came crashing down onto the bed. Then he ran. He ran with every ounce of energy he had left, a thousand things going through his head. The pain of the whip and what Mica must still be feeling from it, how Damian Black could play his mothers death back to him, how Mica's parents had helped him, and how long he had before he was caught if he didn't run fast enough.

He heard footsteps behind him and kicked up his speed a notch, feeling that his legs were actually running faster than the rest of his body and he feared falling. His chest heaved and his throat pinched together. He came busting through the girls' dorm doors like a man on fire, and in one swift movement he ran to Mica's bedside, scooping her up in his arms like a rag doll. Knowing the pain she was in, he propped the Shiva Lingham in her lap and ran into the bathroom, just as Damian Black entered through the doors behind him.

As instructed, all the children were lined up holding hands; the red head cradled Buddha. Mica, draped in Dylan's arms felt a wave of unconsciousness threaten her. The pain of Dylan picking her up was too much, but she fought it, and as they reached the sink and the red-head grabbed Dylan's elbow, connecting them all, Mica submerged the Shiva Lingham into the water, thinking of home, of fresh food, of safety. She thought of Gran, the domes, the steps of Harvard in Boston, and all at once they were being pulled, nauseatingly through a black tunnel. Then somewhere they hit ground.

Nadia, Chloe, and their dad were all in his house near Harvard, standing around the big open living room, which was emptied of furniture per Nadia's request, and only had one table that held thirty-three bag lunches.

"Sweetie, are you sure you saw…" But before Nadia's dad could question her abilities and her odd request, thirty-three kids and a small barking dog appeared three feet above the floor and then all came crashing down.

Mica landed hard and cried out in pain as her backside hit the hardwood floor; she was tangled in Dylan's arms. As she looked up and saw Dr. Culbertson, Chloe, and Nadia, she smiled realizing that the universe really did want to help her. She'd wanted safety, food, and home, and she got exactly that.

They helped the children up, and Chloe and Nadia ran over to Mica.

"Dad, she's hurt!" Chloe screamed.

Their dad was staring in amazement at the sudden appearance of the children. Like he'd thought they would knock on the door or something, not appear out of thin air. He walked over to Mica slowly, looking down at the Shiva Lingham in her hand, arching his eyebrows. Mica looked up. "It's a long story, we're all very hungry, and I need to be alone for a little bit, I'm in a lot of pain and I need to heal myself."

She leaned in towards Dylan. "I know we said we would leave right away, but do you think were safe here for one night? I can heal myself here and be in better shape for traveling." Mica was comforted at the sign of everyone's auras but a little distressed at her own. She knew, if given time she could heal much more easily here than in another world, where she was unsure of her powers. As much as Dylan wanted to get moving to be safe somewhere else, he knew she was in pain and needed to heal herself. This was a best-case scenario, landing in Dr. Culbertson's house and so he nodded yes.

"OK, one night, we leave first thing in the morning."

Chloe and Nadia passed out the lunches while Mica excused herself carrying Buddha down the hall. She went into their father's bathroom, and drew a hot bath with lots of bubbles. There were wheelchair ramps all over the house and Mica was happy to know she had helped Dr. Culbertson to heal and he would no longer need them.

She dipped into the hot bath with pleasure. Something about being in water had always soothed her soul. As she inched into the water, the marks on her back stung and she bit her tongue to keep from crying out. Buddha lay next to the tub sleeping. Mica spread her fingers wide and started charging up the water with healing energy, seeing the golden light pour out of her fingers was such a comforting sign. She'd never tried to heal herself from something this bad, always just a scrape on the knee or a bruise. As she took deep breaths, letting the light flow, it turned the bath water into a soothing baby blue and wrapped itself around her back, already she felt the welts closing. They wouldn't heal completely from this small time she spent on them, but enough to where she could walk around and be comfortable. She swirled her fingers in the bath like a spoon mixing a cake and watched the light absorb into her body. It was so warm and refreshing she felt better already.

Once the water was no longer hot and she felt mildly recovered, she dried off and changed into some clean clothes Nadia and Chloe had waiting for her. As Mica made her way back to the living room she marveled at Nadia's gift. That she had known all of the children would be here, she really was something special and Mica would miss her tomorrow when they had to leave. Part of her wanted Nadia to go too, but knew she wouldn't leave Chloe, and Mica wouldn't want them to get hurt. It had already been so dangerous and she kind of liked them here, safe and waiting.

Mica entered the big room, scuffling her feet on the hardwood floors with Buddha close behind. Dylan was talking to Dr. Culbertson and she paused watching him. He had sacrificed so much for her, they had grown so close and been through so much together. She felt like she had known him for twenty lifetimes. He looked up.

"Hey, feeling better?" he asked. Mica smiled, nodding yes. All of the children greeted Mica with hugs and thanked her for saving them from a life of captive pain. Mica and Dylan passed the time telling Dr. Culbertson, Chloe and Nadia the story of Lady Evil and how they went into the other world and the soul color in their hair and everything. Dr. Culbertson was fascinated by everything, he was amazed that she could travel to other worlds, but not to surprised to learn they existed.

"Mica, you must make me a promise, right here and now." Mica, smiled already knowing what he would say.

"Anything," she replied.

"One day, when all of this is over, you must promise to take me to another world, even for only a second. Just to feel the transition would make my entire life complete." He gazed at her like a child, asking a parent for permission to eat candy.

"I promise."

Chloe seemed to have left her attitude at the door and was actually very protective of Mica, making sure she was okay, if she needed water, making sure no one touched her back too hard. Mica realized being Chloe's enemy was the worst, but it was worth it once she brought you into her circle of friends. It was just too bad she thought you were her enemy from the second you met her.

Dr. Culbertson stood up. "I have an announcement." All of the children quieted. He looked at his daughters, who were gushing with excitement. "In exactly twenty minutes we shall all watch some TV and I have a surprise for Mica." He smiled and Mica wondered what it could be. Then she got an idea and excused herself, but promised to be back in ten minutes so she wouldn't miss the surprise.

She went to the kitchen to a phone that hung on the wall. She picked it up and immediately tears were streaming from her face. She dialed the number and waited anxiously.

"Hello? This is Priscilla?"

"Gran!!!" Mica screamed. She didn't care who heard. The sound of that woman's voice made Mica's heart grow wings.

"Oh, my dear girl, I miss you so much. You shouldn't be calling though, it's not safe."

"I don't care, I needed to hear your voice. Grandpa's dead." There was silence. "But I'm okay. I miss you." Mica added.

"Good, dear, I'm so proud of you. Be safe. Do everything your grandpa said. You're my light and I love you. I'm counting on you."

Mica couldn't find her voice, her throat was in knots. "You too, Gran. I'm going to see you soon, I promise. Everything will be okay, I'm going to fix everything."

Mica hung up the phone and wiped her face, joining the rest of the group in the main room. Dr. Culbertson had the TV on and had situated pillows and cushions on the floor in a u-shape so everyone could see the TV. There were two pillows closest to the TV and Dylan was sitting on one of them. He looked up at her and smiled, patting the empty pillow next to him. Mica blushed at the thought that he had saved a seat for her. She sat next to him, feeling comfort at being so close and absorbing his good energy. They watched the last two minutes of the previous program and then the news came on. "This is it, everyone." Chloe jumped up, turning it louder. Mica, prepared herself for what this could be.

Chapter Eight
Ronak

The TV blared to life, "Hello, Dome City dwellers, welcome to our worldwide broadcast. I'm in Boston and I have hijacked the news station to bring you a bit of information that a certain new World Leader doesn't want to get out." It was Mark Densy, the Harvard class president who had healed the water with Mica!

"I am the class president at Harvard University and I'm a Quantum Physics major. I'm happy to say after years of experiments and research, we have found a way to heal the planet of its pollution and break free of the domes, no longer relying on the failing Nanobot technology. We can cure the virus and once again live on the outside, together. Actually, we found a girl who is leading the way. I introduce to you the one and only, Mica Moon."

The room erupted with clapping.

Mica snapped her head back at the Professor, who was grinning ear to ear. She looked back at the TV, just in time to see an entire taping of her speech at Harvard. It showed her healing Dr. Culbertson's legs, helping Mark to heal the water, and lastly being forcefully pulled out by Damian Black's men. Then it showed Mark back in the studio and you could hear banging on the doors behind him.

"Well, folks, I'm about to go to jail, I'm sure. Just remember, when the sun rises on August 15th, drop to the Earth and give your thanks and love, and know that Mica Moon will be setting us all free. It doesn't matter where in the world you are or if your timing is exactly right, just join with your neighbors and love the Earth again! Freeworld!" His fist shot into the air at those last words and then the door burst open. Damian Black's men ran in, rushing Mark to the floor and knocking over the cameras, Mark was still screaming, but you couldn't see him, just a still-shot of an open door.

He screamed, "See, Mica, didn't kill the late World Leader it's all a lie, Damian Black sends his men to do his evil bidding; their attacking me right now for exposing the truth!" The screen went blue.

Mica slowly turned to look at Dr. Culbertson. "It was the girls' idea." But before he could finish those words Mica rushed at him with a big hug knocking the wind out of him; she turned and hugged the two girls. Chloe spoke, "Now you just keep safe and when it's time, come back here and don't forget about us. Everyone will believe you, we know it." She smiled and Mica was eternally grateful the word had gone out to millions of people and that was better than she could have ever done on her own. In her happiness she also felt more pressure, now it was real, she really had to come through for all of these people.

The TV zipped back to life. A startled blonde reporter was speaking fast with sweat on her brow.

"Well, folks, sorry for that childish interruption. You have just seen a practical joke. The students at Harvard always do such good computer graphics, especially on that video of the little girl, right Tim?"

The male reporter nodded. "Indeed, Maria, now let's get on with the show."

They turned the TV off. The kids tried to reassure Mica people wouldn't believe it was a joke, but she couldn't deny the pit in her stomach. After a few hours of lying around talking with everyone, Mica and Buddha followed Nadia down the hall into her room. It felt like ages since Mica had slept and she was glad when Nadia offered her bed, saying she would sleep with Chloe down the hall. Mica lay down, stroking Buddha with one hand and giving her back more healing energy with the other. After a long while, she drifted off.

Dylan awoke from his dream, knowing he didn't have a second to waste. He ran into the bathroom, plugging the sink and turning on the faucet, then bolted down the hall to where Mica slept. She lay curled in bed, one hand on her back. Buddha jumped up as the door opened.

"Mica, men are coming for us. I had a dream, we need to go now!" Mica jumped up, feeling her heart pounding, the adrenalin rush going to her head. She grabbed Buddha and her purple bag with the Shiva Lingham, and as they came out of the hall, Nadia was waiting for them.

"Good luck, Mica, I'll miss you." Nadia said sleepily.

Mica smiled as Dylan dragged her down the hallway to the bathroom. "Thanks for everything, you're the best!" Mica screamed, already missing her new friend.

In the bathroom, the sink was full. They heard the front door burst open. Mica barely had the Shiva Lingham out of her bag, before Dylan put his hand over hers, thrusting it into the water. She had no time to think of where they should go, this trip was different, it didn't feel like she was falling or being pulled but floating.

After a longer than normal spin into oblivion without the nausea, they softly landed on a pillow and opened their eyes. A man stood before them in an indigo-hooded, long-sleeved robe made of a thick silky fabric. They were in a great stone room shaped like a pyramid. The very point at the top had been cut off so that the sun shone through and beamed into the center.

"Welcome, Mica, welcome, Dylan, I am Ronak." He gave a small bow of his head. Mica tensed at the fact that he knew their names. Dylan reached a protective arm around Mica's shoulders. Buddha jumped on Mica's lap, sensing their fear. But then she realized she could still see auras here and this man was calming and trustworthy with a golden violet aura.

"Do not be afraid, children, this is a land of peace and harmony, no harm can EVER come to you here." His lips weren't moving! Mica looked at Dylan in shock and he in turn had noticed it.

"Oh, yes, I forget how alarming mental telepathy can be at times." This time he spoke out loud. "I shall refrain from doing that until you're ready."

"Where are we?" Dylan asked.

The man was very tall with bony broad shoulders. His hair was blonde, like Mica's, and fell just below his shoulders like long strands of silk. There were tiny braids on each side of his head by his ears. His eyes were wise and sparkled a deep majestic blue. He looked about forty years old but it was hard to tell.

"You are in the original dimension. The very first world ever created. The master world as we like to refer to it. No one may travel hear uninvited. In this world we teach children with potential how to maintain life in other worlds. Our students go on to stop wars, end famine, reverse plague, become World Leaders and so on, they use their gifts to help humans sustain life. Without us, most worlds would not exist."

"So you save people and they don't even know it?" Mica asked.

"Well, in your world when the virus began and the air was really sick and the sun was killing people they wouldn't last much longer without a solution."

"Yes, but then my great-grandfather invented the domes and the Nanobots and we were all saved," Mica added, proud of her historical knowledge.

"Yes, we helped your great-grandfather and your grandfather by giving them the schematic make-up of the domes. We told them about Nanobots, how to make them, and that Nanobots would be able to sense and filter such environmental things as heat, light, and sounds. And that they could also make surface textures, communicate and replicate, and told them how to genetically mutate the food so it would be nourishing and not harmful. Also, I gave you that dream, Dylan, so that you would meet Mica. And, Mica, I led those psychics, Gretta and Nadia, to you." The man smiled sweetly. There was no ego in what he said, just a fact.

"So, then, why have you called us here?" Dylan asked, already knowing the answer.

"I am here to invite you to be students at The Universal School of Lightworkers. Not all children with gifts are invited, only the ones with the purest of hearts, such as yours. I would also like to invite Nadia next time you see her although I know she will not come without her sister and we have no need for Chloe. Nevertheless I must ask. Would you like a tour before you make your decision?"

Mica looked at Dylan, was this really happening? School for the gifted, saving worlds, sometimes it all seemed so crazy, like a movie. But compared to the past week, nothing could really surprise Mica.

Dylan spoke, "Actually we can't make any sort of decision until we've finished a job we have back home. A lot of people are counting on us." Ronak smiled at Dylan.

"See, that is the pure heart I'm talking about. Yes, I am quite aware of the task you have ahead of you and if you decide to enroll in studies here they would not start until after you've saved the people from the virus and the depleting domes. IF you save them." He said this plainly without ill intent, just an observation.

"You mean you don't know if we will?" Mica felt a lump in her throat. At his word "If" she felt despair creeping in.

"Freewill is the master of your destiny, and I do not see one certain outcome, it could go either way at this point." He was not being crude, just honest. Mica's eyes were searching her feet. "Shall we get on with the tour then?" Ronak asked.

Mica and Dylan followed him out of the pyramid, as Buddha trotted behind them into a courtyard. They took in a deep refreshing breath at what they saw. Buddha's eyes squinted in the light. The pyramid seemed to be on a large hill and they were now looking down at a village. There were green weeping willow trees, waterfalls, bright flowers and stone walkways leading to several big buildings with large pillared front steps. They were walking down the pathway when Mica looked down and noticed all the stones had spirals carved in them. Ronak acknowledged her curiosity.

"The schools insignia, the symbol for the evolution of the universe. The school grounds cover a large one hundred and eleven square miles. We have the main learning area with living quarters and classrooms. Then we have a farming section and a large pasture for training games and large group meditations. There are over forty lakes and rivers; we have twenty species of livestock and a small city for staff and apprentice housing. There is also a labyrinth I might take you to sometime; it helps one to find meaning and clarity in the meaningless and unclear."

As he spoke to them a large bird flew from the pyramid at the top of the hill down toward the village about 10 feet over their head. As it approached Dylan realized it wasn't a bird it was a man in a deep blue-hooded sweater. He gasped out loud as he watched the figure float easily through the air.

Ronak smiled. "Levitation. It will be part of your studies here if you decide to come. I did forget how much fun it is to have new students. Everything is so exciting to them."

He took them further down the path, until a thicket of dense trees spread out. They walked under a white lattice trellis into a main courtyard, which had four circle stone buildings all facing each other. In the middle was an immensely large water fountain. On the front of each building was an engraving.

"Earth, Air, Water and Fire." Ronak said. "Each one is a tribal habitat for the children who are grouped according to their soul element."

"How do you group people? Which tribe would I be in? " Mica asked transfixed.

"Well you group yourselves actually. You tell me what you see in the middle of the courtyard." Ronak smiled; this was indeed his favorite part of taking on new students.

Mica squinted for over a minute, looking for some kind of bird on the fountain or another symbol that maybe no one else saw. After two full minutes she threw up her hands. "I don't know I just see the fountain."

Ronak nodded. "And you Dylan what do you see?"

Dylan had been looking with Mica, and he too only saw the fountain.

"The same, nothing else is there." Dylan replied.

Ronak laughed, he really did take pleasure in this.

"Well, to some there's a great big copper bowl holding a large flame of fire that's flickering in the air." Mica and Dylan widened their eyes in surprise.

"Therefore you both are grouped into the water tribe. Whatever element is in your soul is displayed at all times in this courtyard, whether it's a water fountain, a bowl of fire, a small mountain of Earth or a large ornate wind chime, the universe needs all four to be balanced and complete. I see them all of course. Let's move along, shall we?"

"Wait, how can you see them all?" Mica asked.

"That's a conversation for another day."

Mica was starting to think Ronak was immortal. Surely not, but she was definitely going to ask him until he answered, how he could see all four. Ronak was already walking away with Dylan, so Mica ran to catch up.

Mica and Dylan were amazed at everything he showed them over the next hour. Classrooms made of crystal walls for crystal healing studies, children trying to levitate off a hill and dropping ten feet to the ground falling on there backside, and he even showed them a class of aura reading and mental telepathy. He said there were many more, but those were the basic first year studies. He also told them that each spirit group had a special thing in their dorm to connect their souls with their element. The water spirit dorm had a huge saltwater pool filled with a family of six dolphins so they could regenerate and swim with dolphins. Mica had never seen a dolphin so she was really excited. Then they came to a great long building with a figure eight symbol on it, tilted to the side.

"The symbol for eternity." Ronak said.

"This is were the food is eaten and the great meetings are held and the children study." As they made their way through the large glass doors, they noticed there were four oversized circle tables, each one had a floating sign overhead, one symbol was a mountain, one was a flame, another swirls and lastly waves. They were carved deep into the wood of the sign.

They walked over to the water table and about eighty children were eating there. Ronak walked past the table over to a long buffet and grabbed a plate.

"Hungry?" he asked. They were and so Dylan and Mica stocked their plates full of sandwiches and fruit and salad. Mica grabbed a few pieces of chicken for Buddha. Everything looked very healthy, and Dylan was a little upset there were no cookies or brownies. Ronak sensed his disappointment. "Our bodies are a vessel and we must take care of them, even though we have gifts we are human and must be healthy." Dylan smirked at that, but was too hungry to argue.

As they approached the table a few kids called greetings to Ronak, bowing their heads.

"These are two new recruits, thinking of joining The Universal School of Lightworkers. Any words of encouragement?" Ronak asked the children.

One boy spoke up with a grin. "Yeah, make sure you cushion your backside before levitation class." Frowning, he rubbed his bottom with his hand. Mica and Dylan laughed, wondering if he was the one they saw falling earlier.

They set their plates down and grabbed their sandwiches. "Stop," said Ronak in a commanding tone.

Mica and Dylan froze. Ronak closed his eyes and held his hands over his food. He opened one eye and tipped his head, ushering Mica and Dylan to do the same, they then held their palms over their plates. Mica could see violet energy flowing from his hands to his food and she followed suit, giving the food healing energy. Dylan unknowingly did the same with a golden light bathing his sandwich that only Mica could see; she smiled at his natural healing ability.

Ronak began to speak, "Thank you, Mother Earth, for your grain and thank you to the animal that died so I could have nourishment. I know many in the worlds go without meals today and I am grateful for this food. May it balance my body and give me energy." Dylan screwed up his face at that, not really wanting to think about the animal that had died for his food, but thought it was a nice thing to say. So Mica and Dylan said the same.

"Okay, lets eat." Mica swore the food tasted richer than ever and wondered if it was because they had given thanks for it. It was almost like the food was conscious and was returning the thanks by being extra tasty.

After the meal Ronak led them back to the courtyard with the four dorms and the giant fountain in the middle. He stood, overlooking the fountain a ways off and turned to them. "Dylan your gift of sight and dreams and courage would be a great help to the universe. You have untapped powers that we would like to help you explore. Mica, your gift of healing and communication and your tender heart would change the way of the worlds forever. Would you both accept the council of the Elders invitation and begin your training here after your task is complete?"

Mica asked him for a moment alone to talk to Dylan, and Ronak obliged, walking a little ways off.

"Oh, Dylan, I want to come back here and do this, don't you? It feels meant to be."

"Yeah, it all makes sense that there would be a master world and that our gifts wouldn't go to waste after we heal the domed world. I'll stay with you. I'll follow you anywhere, you know that. We're in this craziness together." Dylan said smiling.

Mica smiled in return, feeling nervous and excited all at the same time. She felt whole.

"I guarantee that life at school here will ensure that we will never be bored." Mica stated.

"I think you're right. Crystal rooms, levitation, pyramids, and labyrinths, I think we're in for some excitement." Dylan agreed.

They walked back over to Ronak. "We will accept," Mica said, "but Buddha must stay as well."

"I wouldn't dream of splitting you two apart, he is a very special dog." Buddha barked and they all laughed.

Ronak looked up at the sun knowing the time. "Well, right on time for our meeting with the council of the Elders to induct you."

"What do you mean right on time? You knew we would say yes?" Mica asked.

"Yes, yes, I did," He said with a smile. Mica liked him very much she knew she could learn a lot from Ronak and wondered what world he was from. They walked back up the spiral stone pathway to the temple where they first came. At the door Ronak paused and closed his eyes. Mica saw his aura and when his eyes closed, a light like a wave burst from his head and rippled out and just then someone came to the door. "Louder than knocking." He winked at Mica.

"Welcome, Ronak, children." A small woman with a pale pink, silk, hooded, long sleeve jacket nodded courteously to them.

"Thank you, Reva." Ronak said.

Reva bowed and left through a corridor, she was clearly an assistant. This time they entered the giant room to see a long table with twelve people sitting around it facing them. The walls had engravings of the spiral and many more symbols Mica couldn't figure out. As they approached the table, Mica felt a deep sense that they were in the presence of powerful people. Her eyes burned at the sight of their combined aura energy and she had to turn her head and not look directly into the fierce glow. She took a breath, toning down her power, and looked back. There were six men and six women in all. They all sat tall and proud wearing a multitude of indigo-shaded hooded sweaters. The women's sweaters were beaded and shimmered silk while the men's were stiff cotton and had big deep hoods lined with violet satin and fitted sleeves. They all had embroidered spirals on their chest.

"Mica Moon, please step forward," said the man to the far left. Mica looked at Ronak who nodded her forward.

Mica walked forward a few feet and bowed her head slightly feeling it the right show of respect.

A woman in the middle spoke.

"We are the council of Elders and we're very pleased at your acceptance into The Universal School of Lightworkers. We have great hopes for you and our good grace and wishes go with you on your task to heal your world back home. Upon return from your trip, whether you pass or fail your people, you will be greeted with open arms. You are always welcome here and you must know how special you are. Dark forces are at work to see you fail and so we hold you in the light."

"Thank you." It's the only thing Mica could think of to say.

"May I see the Shiva Lingham?" she asked.

Mica froze for a second at the randomness of her question. She recovered quickly and pulled it from her bag, trusting this woman completely. Mica handed her the stone and she rolled it in her hands and held it up to the beam of the light coming through the pyramid. She glanced at the other Elders and nodded deeply.

"Mica, all universal world travel is overseen and guided by us. The only exceptions are those who own a Shiva Lingham and are powerful enough to morph it into a traveling device. Aside from yours, only one other exists and it belongs to Damian Black." Mica recoiled at the mention of his name.

"He was a student here many years ago with your grandfather and they both went on to become great beings of supernatural power. Your grandfather, however, was the only one able to hold the light within himself, while Damian succumbed to the darkness and ego of his power. Every student that is invited here is met in their world and brought here by a traveler, a person with our permission to travel worlds. We do not let people keep these devices, as they can be dangerous to the universe in the wrong hands. Nevertheless, we have foreseen that it is a part of your destiny and will allow you to keep it. The energy signature your great-great grandfather put on it only allows those with a pure heart to use it, but nevertheless it must not ever leave your possession and you must not tell other students about it." She handed Mica back the stone.

"OK," Mica said in compliance.

A man on the far corner of the table smiled at Mica. "Open your palms please and approach the table."

Mica opened her hands and walked closer. She reached the person on the far left and they grabbed her palms holding them open in front like a book. Mica thought they were reading them until she saw the woman trace a spiral onto each palm, light was flooding out of her hands as she did this. Mica felt her hair stand up, and as she walked to the right each Elder placed a symbol onto her palm, until she reached the last person. He stood, drawing waves onto her hands and said, "I declare you a water spirit, may your soul be calm and soothing and may you be a steadfast force for the universe, bringing waves of peaceful healing energy."

Just then Mica felt like waves of water were rushing up her arms. After a moment, she stood back to join Ronak and Dylan.

"Dylan Pierce, please step forward." This time a man in the middle wearing a deep indigo blue hood addressed him. Dylan stepped forward.

"Mica, put out a call to the universe for help and you answered. You are a loyal friend and a worthy lightworker. You have a very important destiny, but it is not your task to save the people from the domed world and heal the Earth, in the end only Mica can do it and we give you a chance now to be free from that burden. If you choose, you may wait here until Mica has finished her task. We warn you that if you go, we foresee danger, and it is not your destiny to accompany her."

Mica felt a lump in her throat at the thought of doing it all alone, but Dylan spoke without hesitation.

"I will not leave her, she needs my help, and I'm here to offer it at any cost." The man looked to the other Elders nodding his head and then he bowed his head slightly to Dylan.

"Very well then, we wish you blessings and respect you for going on this journey. Please come forward for the symbol initiation."

Dylan stepped forward replaying the man's words in his head *"we foresee danger"* danger to Mica or just him? He stepped forward nervously, and as soon as the first woman drew on his hands, he felt a wave of encouragement and calmness enter his spirit. As he reached the man at the end, he also declared Dylan a water spirit but just before Dylan was about to walk away, the man grabbed his shoulders bringing him close to his face. The crystal in Dylan's hair was vibrating.

The man whispered in Dylan's ear and placed one hand on Dylan's forehead.

"I place a bubble of protection around your body, may it keep you safe in times of peril, preserving your essence throughout all levels and dimensions." He then let go and nodded. Dylan felt different, unexplainably different. He looked at the man perplexed.

He walked backward, thinking of everything that had been said, they all bowed and made their way outside with Ronak. Mica asked what the man had whispered to him. Dylan didn't have the heart to tell her, for he feared that just by following her to the domed world he was putting his life in jeopardy, but he just couldn't let her do it alone.

"Just initiation stuff, ya know? That was cool, huh?" Dylan replied. Mica looked at his aura he was hiding something but she decided not to press him, it was probably just something private or embarrassing. "Yeah, that was cool, I'm glad we're both water spirits, that means we will both live in the same tribal dorm."

They walked in silence back down to the dorms with Ronak, initiation seemed to leave one to their thoughts. Even Ronak seemed lost in thought.

As they reached the fountain, Ronak spoke, "Okay, you will spend the next two nights here and prepare for the school year and then I shall help you travel back to your world."

"Umm, oh, actually we need to head a bit farther west before we can go back, because Damian Black will be looking for me in Boston, and we have over a month before we need to get back in time for the healing. And not to be rude, but we don't really need your help traveling, we have the Shiva Lingham, remember?" Mica smiled very proud of her plan not meaning any offense.

Ronak smiled back at her.

"Well, ACTUALLY, this world is only big enough to hold the school grounds. There is no farther west here and you do need my help traveling because I'm going to drop you off in Sedona in the future, the night before you are to heal that world." Mica and Dylan exchanged a look.

"Oh," Mica said, "well, thank you." Ronak patted her back, such a pure soul, so naive, he thought. He had walked them over to the water tribe dorms a great big wooden sign hung above the door with the wave insignia. He opened the doors. "I leave you here, enjoy your time in this world, it is a place of rest and recuperation for your spirit, and you will need it for the task ahead."

"Thanks for everything, Ronak." Dylan said to the tall man, feeling that he would miss his presence.

"Wait," Mica said "Will we see you a lot in school? I mean are you our teacher or anything?" Mica had begun to like the man and his comforting wise words and wondered what role he would play throughout their studies.

"My dear children, you can never escape me. I am your spirit guide." He smiled boldly thinking these two apprentices worthy of his guidance and enjoying their curiosity.

As Ronak turned away, he floated up into the air, levitating perfectly and headed back towards the temple. Mica and Dylan smiled at each other still in awe at the sight of a grown man gliding through the air.

Chapter Nine
The Universal School of Lightworker's

They were still in the doorway, watching Ronak leave when a woman spoke to them.

"New initiates over here please, orientation has begun!" The woman wore a light peach, hooded silk sweater with gold spiral embroidery on the sleeves, which draped and hung to her waist almost like a Japanese kimono. She waved them over looking a bit flustered.

She was about twenty feet away, across the main common room, holding open two double doors into a meeting room. She raised her eyes, tipping her head. "Hurry please." Mica and Dylan ran towards her with Buddha trotting along.

"I'll take the dog to be washed and fed, okay?" The woman scooped up Buddha in one swift movement and looked at Mica.

"Alright, I guess that's OK," Mica swatted Buddha's head quickly with a little tap. "Go with her Buddha it's alright." Mica and Dylan turned to face the room. It had long rows of benches full of children and at the front, a woman and a man in silver hoods stood in front of a large spiral sculpture and a wooden wave sign hung above them.

Mica and Dylan took two seats towards the back.

"Welcome, water spirits!" the woman shouted. "We are so happy to have you here at The Universal School of Lightworkers."

The woman had a beautiful aura. She was very motherly and Mica liked her at once. "I am Mentor Kolara and this is Mentor Dane. We are your water spirit tribe leaders and teachers for some of your studies. Since it is your first year here your uniforms will be white-hooded sweaters with a gold embroidery of the water spirit insignia. Or 'hoodies' as the children are referring to them nowadays." All the children laughed and she smiled and went on.

"As you progress in school here the color of your hoodies progress. Second years wear orange hoodies, third years wear green and fourth years wear blue. Spirit guides and other highly evolved souls including the council of Elders wear an indigo-colored hoodie. I should hope that some of you would be adorned with that color one day. All teachers wear silver hoodies and other staff wear pink, peach or yellow. The color is just a way of identifying, but everyone is created equal and special in their own right. I trust you all had a pleasant time meeting with your spirit guides?" The children murmured in agreement.

She went on, "They will be with you for the rest of your studies here and on into your adulthood whenever you need them. Each spirit guide has one student for life, and THEY pick YOU, based on your abilities so you should feel very special and know that it was not random; they all chose to guide you for a reason. In some very special cases one spirit guide can have two students. Throughout the rest of your life, just call on them and they will be there. If they have chosen you it's because they believe in you and are here to help you on your life path." Mica was surprised at this, wondering how Ronak had known anything about them and thought it interesting that she and Dylan had the same one.

The man now stepped forward smiling. "The Universal School of Lightworkers has been around far longer than any of our human minds can compute. It was established in the beginning of creation by the Source to monitor progress in other worlds and to teach those with pure hearts and special gifts to help others sustain life. Most worlds operating today are running on a low frequency.

After your studies here, if you are chosen, you will go to a world in need and raise their vibrational frequency to that of a healthy peaceful place. People act out of love more often at this high frequency and the world responds better, lasting longer. Depending on your gift, you may go with a group of graduates to establish this frequency. You are all here because you possess some special power, whether you're a Traveler, Telepath, Healer, Levitator, or a Manifestor, our goal here is to teach you to harness all of the five gifts and become a true worker of the light. That being said, you will never be as good at the other gifts as you are with your natural talent. We only teach you to tap into the other gifts in a small way, but it's always best to seek healing from a natural healer or travel with a natural traveler." The man squinted his eyes, looking straight at Mica.

"I see some of you here today possess more than one gift naturally, that is rare and we're very pleased to have you." He nodded, standing back and inviting Mentor Kolara to step forward again. Every pair of eyes turned and scanned in Mica and Dylan's direction, whispering about who could possess more than one gift.

"So, classes begin Monday, and you can pick up your schedules from your spirit guides, they know what classes you can handle. Each of you has a room in the dormitories. Your names as well as your roommate's names are engraved over the door so you can find your rooms. In the back of the Eternity hall where we all share our meals there is a supply store, where you can meet many of your basic needs. Tonight we will feast there in celebration of the new students. I live at the end of the hall in the girls dorm and Mentor Dane lives at the end of the hall in the boys', so if you need anything, just ask. Many blessings, peace be with you." She smiled, and with that the kids grabbed their bags of belongings and started walking toward the exits, talking excitedly of the new school year.

Dylan turned to Mica, "We don't have any clothes or much money for books. These kids brought proper suitcases full of stuff." Mica was used to his English accent by now but it was still funny when he said "proper".

"I'm sure we will figure it out. Lets check out our rooms!" Mica said excitedly.

Mica found her room and was both sad and relieved to see that she didn't have a roommate. The sign above her door read (Mica and Buddha). She opened the door and was stunned at all the things in the room. She scanned the room taking it all in. To the right, stood a small twin bed, lavishly decorated with light blue and silver bed linens and extra pillows. To the left was another bed but without the linens, since she didn't have a roommate but as Mica looked back at her bed it had an aura! Mica stood perplexed at this, until she walked over and pulled up the top mattress. Underneath, where the box spring should have been was a rectangular stand with beautifully inlayed crystals and a silver plaque that read,

"This crystal healing bed will regenerate your spirit and expand your mind. Namaste." Namaste? What did that mean? She made a mental note to ask Ronak. Crystals had always given off a certain energy imprint to Mica, but this was amazing it looked like the entire bed was glowing; she fantasized about how grand it would be to sleep immersed in this exquisite energy.

There must have been two hundred small polished stones and they were set in a silver plaster that almost looked like glitter. Mica was proud of her knowledge of crystals as she recognized most of the stones she saw. There was rose quartz, lapis lazuli, carnelian, amethyst, selenite, pearl, hematite, ruby and even chunks of mica.

In the back of the room, between the two beds, there was a large doghouse, four feet tall, for Buddha, and a doggie door leading outside to a patch of grass where he could go to the bathroom! As Mica drew closer to the house, Buddha came running out wagging his tail. He wore a new collar; it was indigo and a crystal hung from it. Next to the crystal was a star-shaped tag. On one side it read, "Buddha, Water Spirit." On the other, it bore the schools' spiral insignia. Buddha's fur was fluffy and soft. "Boo, you haven't been this clean in ages!" He yipped around the room and ran into his house. Mica laughed. She crawled into the house with him and saw a little bed with toys and food and water; there were symbols at the bottom of the water bowl and one looked like a bunch of overlapping sevens with two dots. Mica wondered what all of these symbols meant.

After a few minutes Mica eased out of the doghouse and went over to the dresser, noticing a note on top. *"Sometimes those of us with few possessions are richer in spirit. Even so, this should be everything you should need. –Ronak"* Mica opened the drawers, which were full of clothes, undergarments, white hoodies, socks, and even two pair of shoes sat at the bottom on the floor. Mica was deeply appreciative.

Mica went to use the bathroom and was startled by the sight of a little girl washing her hands.

"Oh, I'm sorry!" Mica said retreating.

"No, no, it's okay, we're suite mates, we share a bathroom. Come on in, I'm just washing my hands." The girl was extremely short and had wild curly red hair, at least twice the size of her head in volume, and it reached to just below her neck. She dried off on a towel and held her hand out in greeting. "Teensie. Nice to meet you."

"Teensie? Is that your name?" Mica was confused as to why someone would name their child Teensie. For such a small thing, the girl laughed heartily. "I was premature and only weighed three pounds at birth. I guess my parents have a sense of humor. I'm fourteen, although I know I look eleven."

Mica smiled, it was rather funny. "I'm Mica. I was named after a rock."

They both laughed and shook hands becoming instant friends.

"What's your sign?" Teensie asked.

"My sign? Oh, I'm a water sprit like you."

The girl howled in laughter. "No, your astrological sign? I'm a Sagittarius."

"Oh, I dunno, my birthday is January 30th," Mica replied.

"Oh great! An Aquarius, we will be good friends! I told the school there was no way I would be suite mates with a Virgo or Scorpio. Aquarius was my first choice! No wonder you're a water spirit, your sign is that of the water bearer."

"Oh, I don't know anything about astrology." Mica admitted.

"Then I shall have to teach you! Can I see your room?" Teensie walked past Mica without an answer.

Buddha ran out to greet them. Mica showed Teensie all around her room, and Teensie marveled at the doghouse. "I have a pet cat back home, but I couldn't bring him. So your dog must be special." She didn't seem jealous, just upset at the thought of her cat.

"He is special, I saved him from dying and I've had him since I was little." Buddha hung his head low at the memory.

"So what's your gift? I can travel. One day I hope to be a traveler for the Elders going on missions and stuff. Knowing astrology helps me, because I can align the planets and universes in my head so I don't get lost." Teensie said, obviously having forgotten about her cat.

"That's amazing," Mica said, thinking of how it must be to travel without the Shiva Lingham. "I can see auras and heal with energy, no big deal compared to traveling worlds," Mica said.

"No big deal! Oh my gosh! I've heard about aura seers but never met one, only a few exist. We learn to see auras here at school, but it takes a long time and you never really see them like the naturals do. What color is mine?" Teensie closed her eyes and squinted her face, concentrating. Mica laughed hard out loud.

"Well, just relax, you don't need to close your eyes."

Teensie opened them in excitement. Mica focused on Teensie's aura. It was orange around her body and then became pure white at the tip of her head. She actually resembled the Buddhist monk's aura with a little orange added, not everyone could achieve the pure white halo around their head. That meant Teensie was a very intellectual thinker.

"Well, orange surrounds your body, which means you're excited and have high energy, and probably you're artistic, then around your head it's pure white, which means you're a deep thinker and you use your mind very intensely, probably when you travel to other worlds."

Teensie opened her mouth in shock. "That's amazing. I paint! I am artistic and you're right I do think a lot and I'm very high energy, come see my art! And meet my Aries roommate." Teensie charged out of the room, pulling Mica and Buddha behind her. Mica enjoyed Teensie's company, though after an hour of hanging out with her and her roommate Lexi, she found herself drained and excused herself.

After taking a bath, Mica stood for a long time in front of the mirror. She just looked at herself, wondering if she looked as different as she felt. In just a few weeks she had escaped Damian Black, traveled to other worlds, been beaten, and enrolled in a gifted school. She realized at the thought of being beaten that her back no longer hurt and as she turned to look in the mirror she saw that the welts were completely healed, although they'd left faint pink slashes across her back. Mica wondered if they would be there forever.

She brushed her long platinum hair, thinking of how much she looked like a female Ronak. She didn't meet a lot of natural white hairs and with the pale skin and blue eyes sometimes she felt odd staring in the mirror. She giggled at the idea of braiding the sides of her hair to look like Ronak's and decided against it. She got ready for dinner, pulling on her white hoodie and set off to the boys' dorms to find Dylan. She stood at the doorway, not sure what to do, and then noticed a phone on the wall. It had a numerical list beside it. She located Dylan Pierce and dialed the number unsure, who would answer.

"Hello?" Dylan answered hesitantly.

"Hey," Mica said, "I'm outside if you want to walk down to dinner a bit early and get our books."

Dylan met Mica at the doors. He looked quite handsome in his long white hoodie, which contrasted his dark thick hair, the green moldavite crystal hung in one of his braids and reflected onto his face. Mica noticed his aura looked different ever since he'd come out of the initiation. It was more contained not so big.

"Ronak got me a bunch of clothes and a toothbrush and everything," Dylan said.

"Me, too, and I think there will be books waiting for us as well. He seems to have thought of everything."

They made their way to the Eternity Hall and found the store, packed full of students wearing white hoodies. They got their starter kits, which were huge heavy book bags full of stuff, and it was all free of charge, because Ronak had set up an account for them. The bags bore the water wave logos and schedules were stapled onto the front. Mica ripped hers off, making her way out of the store with Dylan. She read her schedule aloud.

Mica Moon

<u>Spirit Guide: Ronak</u>

1. Beginners' Levitation (Level One)

2. Dream Interpretations and Mind Reading (Level One)

3. The Universe and Travel (Level One)

4. Advanced Aura Reading and Healing with Energy (Level Three)

5. Manifesting (Level Two)

6. History of the Worlds and Creation (Level One)

"Whoa, cool what does your say?" Mica said and Dylan handed his schedule to her.

Dylan Pierce

<u>Spirit Guide: Ronak</u>

1. Beginners' Levitation (Level One)

2. Dream Interpretations and Mind Reading (Level Three)

3. The Universe and Travel (Level One)

4. Aura Reading and Healing with Energy (Level One)

5. Manifesting (Level one)

6.Top Secret (Report to Pyramid)

"Top secret! I wonder what that is? Why aren't I in it?" Mica asked. Dylan peeked over her shoulder to see what she was talking about.

"I don't know what it is. So we have every class together except for a few. I guess whatever your gift is you get moved up to the advanced level," Dylan wondered aloud.

"Top Secret," she repeated, wanting badly to know what that meant.

The crystal in Dylan's ear shook and he arched his eyebrows listening, it whispered, *"Nadia wants you to know they are all okay and she will contact you later."* Mica noticed the change in Dylan's aura when he concentrated and received messages. She was growing used to this.

"What's happening?" Mica asked.

"Nadia wants us to know they're all okay and she'll contact me later, I guess."

"Whoa, she can talk to you like that? Cool."

Dylan smiled, "I guess so."

After dropping off their bags at the dorms, they found a seat next to Teensie at the water spirit tribe table in the Eternity Hall. All the tables were decorated with colors: blue for water, brown for Earth, red for fire, and silver for air. Mica introduced Dylan and they looked around excitedly. Mica was marveling at the different colored hoodies thinking of the four years. Then she realized she didn't know much about school here besides what they'd said at orientation.

"Teensie, how long do we go here before we graduate? Four years, right?" Mica inquired.

"Well, some never graduate. If you don't show promise after a year, they send you home. If you stay it's a four year course and then you get your first apprenticeship."

"Oh, what's an apprenticeship?"

"Well after you graduate, you would apprentice under a healer and go on real missions to help people, and then you can decide whether you want to be a healer for the Elders or become a spirit guide. Or there's this one thing I heard about, you can become a Creator, but that's rare. You have to be invited or something."

"What is a Creator?" Dylan asked, perking up.

"I shouldn't really talk about it, but a Creator helps the Elders to create new worlds!" Teensie spoke the last part as if it were sacred.

"How do you know for sure?" Mica asked.

"I overheard my mom talking to Ronak once, when he used to be an Elder and send her on missions."

"What! Ronak was an Elder?" Dylan blurted out.

"Yeah, but he stepped down to become your spirit guide, it was a huge controversy but he insisted." Teensie said slamming her fist on the palm of her hand to emphasize the word.

"So, Ronak chose to be our spirit guide instead of an Elder?" Mica asked amazed.

"Yep, They say a guide is the most selfless job you can take, you make more of a difference by vowing to teach others. I'm going to be a famous traveler for the Elders, though." Teensie exclaimed.

"How do you know all of this?" Dylan asked.

"My mom went here, she's a traveler too, she'll be our Universe and Travel teacher," Teensie said, smiling proudly.

"So, did you grow up always knowing about this place?" Mica wondered.

"Oh, yeah! My mom would travel here every day to teach and then travel back home in time for dinner. One day, when I was six, I tried to follow her, but ended up in some weird world and the Elders had to send her to rescue me." Teensie spoke about this very proudly, unaware how nerve-wracking it must have been for her mother.

"What's your astro sign, Dylan?" Teensie asked.

"Um, I don't know. My birthday is January 30th," He answered, as Mica sprang up in her seat.

"What. Me too! That's the exact same day." Mica realized she really didn't know much about Dylan's past.

"Really? The same day? That's weird," Dylan said and wondered if it was coincidence.

"Cool. Two Aquarians, I'm so lucky! If you were a Virgo I might have had to move down a few seats."

"What's wrong with Virgos?"

"Shhh. Don't even get me started! My guide says I shouldn't judge people based on their signs, but I'll tell you what, I never met a Virgo I liked, they're always cleaning, they're perfectionists and nit-picking complainers! They can never be true friends and will abandon you in a heartbeat. You're so lucky you're a worthy Aquarius." Dylan widened his eyes at Mica as they shared a thought about how crazy Teensie sounded.

"What if one day when you have kids you have a Virgo, are you going to send it back?" Dylan asked.

"No! I'm going to plan and make sure that doesn't happen! Such a horrid thing to say that I would be plagued with a Virgo." Mica and Dylan laughed. Teensie was dead serious about this astrology stuff.

A boy was approaching and came right up to Mica and Dylan.

"Hey, Dylan, can I sit here?"

"Oh, hey Luke! This is Mica and Teensie. He is my roommate, he's a levitator." Luke was tall with a muscular build. He had short sandy hair and deep soulful brown eyes.

"Hey, guys nice to meet ya. I'm not a levitator yet, I can only get about five feet off the ground," he said modestly.

"That's more than we can do! Sit next to me," Teensie said winking at Mica. Mica thought that maybe Teensie had developed such an outgoing personality to make up for her small size. It was a nice mix to Mica's calm energy. Just as Luke sat down, there was commotion at the front of the room.

The Elders piled in one by one, sitting at a Grand table with high-backed dark wooden chairs, there were hundreds of white tea light candles all around the room and they reflected off their indigo silk hoodies. The children were silenced in the presence of these great beings.

"Welcome, young new spirits. May your white hoodies symbolize purity and the beginning of your journey. We are glad to have you here and hope one day you can give back to the universe by using the knowledge you learned at The Universal School of Lightworkers. We will not always be here to eat meals with you, only on special occasions, as we are usually needed elsewhere. But tonight we dine with you in pleasure and drink to your gifts and pure hearts." The woman speaking was looking right at Mica, smiling. They all raised their glasses to the heartfelt toast.

"One more thing before we eat. Two of you join us tonight with heavy hearts for you have a great task before you. We ask now for a moment of silence and for everyone in the room to send good thoughts to these two brave souls." Mica and Dylan's faces reddened. Everyone closed their eyes and Mica was blinded by the energy output she saw. Even though the children didn't know to whom to send their energy, it gravitated in the air towards Mica and Dylan. They both felt giddy at the reaction.

After a moment the woman spoke again. "Thank you, let's eat! Peace be with you all and don't forget to thank your food." The woman sat down, and Mica's tribe got up first and went over to the buffet.

They dined for two hours, chatting about their lives back home and the new school year. Then an Elder man got up to speak, "Ceremony is important to establish intentions. Tonight's intention has been about welcoming you and now we would like to embrace your elements with a tribal performance. The third and fourth year students will be performing the element embracing ceremony.

You're in for a treat. Enjoy." The man smiled warmly in anticipation of this special event.

Behind the Elders' table at the back of the hall was an elevated stage. A boy in a sage green hoodie walked out, carrying a black leather whip. He was Native American and had the most beautiful long brown braid Mica had ever seen. He wore a leather cuff on his right hand that peeked out beneath his robe. He stood in front of everyone, seemingly floating above the Elders. They had turned around in their chairs to watch.

"Fire," the boy breathed, and the whip came to life. It blazed with red-hot flames. He cracked it and a loud bang resounded throughout the Eternity Hall. At that sound, three other fire spirits raced onto the stage with balls of fire, which hung from metal chains. The students spun them around like batons. They circled the boy with the whip, and he cracked it again as it lurched behind him threatening to singe his beautiful braid. Mica was in awe.

Then four students dropped from the ceiling tangled in nylon ropes. The girl in the middle hung upside down over the boy with the whip and said, "Air." She blew on his whip, sending the flames dancing higher and higher. She gracefully untangled and stood next to him as he twirled the whip in circles, then the other air students dropped from their ropes and blew on the other fire spirits' fire sending the flames ten feet high.

Two girls in blue hoodies came from behind the curtain with leather sacks around their necks. They reached in and threw fistfuls of sand into the flames making them spark and flicker.

"Earth," the girl said, grabbing two more handfuls and placing her open palms in front of the air sprits. They all blew on her hands and a small spiraling tornado arose, turning the sand into a long horn shape that touched the ceiling.

Mica's eyes darted all around, watching the spinning fire balls, the ten-foot flames from the whip, and the swirling sand. Then a huge five-foot deep glass bowl full of water lowered from the ceiling being levitated over the ceremony. Ten water spirits ran out from behind the curtain with drums strapped to their waists. They were beating and pounding on the drums and the vibrations sent waves through the water.

The air spirits blew harder, sending the sand and flames higher, and the water spirits drummed, running in a circle around the entire stage, the low rhythmic beating of the drums grew louder and louder. Mica felt something inside of her resonate with the tribal beating of these drums. Then the water in the bowl rippled so fast, and hard, the bowl cracked in half. The water came rushing down, covering all of the students, and putting out the fires. The bowl hung suspended in mid air, not one shard of glass fell. Some levitators stood off the stage and had it all suspended in mid air. The drumming stopped.

"Water," a drummer boy proclaimed.

Every student, teacher and Elder shot into the air, screaming with joy and clapping loudly.

The levitators eased the large pieces of glass down to the ground. All of the ceremony students took a bow smiling. The Elders stood bowing and then spoke to the tribes.

"Now you see how the four elements can work together. Very nice job! We hope your school year is filled with joy and learning. Namaste." He bowed deeply to the students, who tipped their heads back in respect. Mica, Dylan, Luke and Teensie made their way out of the Eternity Hall and back towards the dorm.

Chapter Ten
The Akashic Records

On their way back to the dorms, the older Native American boy in the sage green hoodie approached Mica, Dylan, Teensie and Luke. The fire symbol was embroidered on his sweater and his long braid swooshed in the air as he walked.

"Hi, I'm Keno, I'm a telepath. After the Elders said two people needed good thoughts I kind of picked up on what was going on, and I wanted to run over and thank you guys for what you're going to do in the domed world. I'm from there and my parents live there, so I'm really relieved to know they will have a better place to be in once you're done healing it." He bowed his head to Mica and brought out his hand to Dylan. Dylan shook it nervously.

"Oh, I'm not really doing anything, it's all her," Dylan said nodding at Mica. The boy frowned slightly.

"We'll see about that. Good luck to both of you." he smiled.

"Thanks. Nice performance, I thought your hair was going to catch fire." Mica said.

"A little secret," he leaned into Mica, and whispered in her ear. Mica laughed and the boy pulled away smiling.

"See you guys soon." Keno said, trotting off.

Dylan looked at Mica waiting for her to tell them what Keno said, but she simply started walking back to the dorms. She was lost in her thoughts, reminded of what a huge deal her task was.

Here they were in another world and people knew about the big healing. Teenise, of course, insisted they fill her and Luke in, so they did, all except for the Shiva Lingham and their other worldly travels. Teensie was loud and animated about the whole thing, which made Mica smile.

After saying goodnight, Mica lay in her bed, feeling her body loosen up on the crystal healing bed. Buddha lay on her stomach, breathing in sync with her. After only a moment, she drifted off into the realm of slumber. She dreamt that she was back in the domed world, on top of a twenty-story building with Dylan; they stood there, and out of nowhere, Damian Black levitated and snatched up Dylan, dropping him over the edge. Mica ran after him, leaping off the edge without a single fear, and as she struck the pavement, she jerked awake. Her pulse beat wildly and as it slowed down she looked at the clock, 3 a.m. She lay back down, trying to regulate her breathing, and drifted back off until ten in the morning. Mica had always been a sleeper. She hated getting up too early, and often needed more than eight hours to feel normal.

After getting ready for the day, she took Buddha for a long walk around the school grounds. She let her mind unravel the ball of clustered ideas. She pulled the hood of her sweater over her head and her white hair peeked out the bottom. Mica was so grateful for all the clothes Ronak gave her. The hoodies were beautiful, like works of wearable art, each one had geometric embroideries either on the sleeve or hood, almost like a repeating mandala. Mica marveled at everyone's hoodies, noticing they all seemed a bit different and wondered if each was one of a kind.

She had always known she was different than other kids and that her gift to see auras and to heal was special, but never in a million years did she think her life's purpose and soul reason for living included saving the world. Then to go on to school and save other worlds she didn't even know existed. Only fourteen, she couldn't even drive or get into a bar, but was entrusted with the fate of millions of people?

And yet, when she thought about not having her power and being normal, she couldn't conceive of happiness that way. This is who she'd become: someone who liked helping people. She thought of Dylan, the spark on their first meeting, the same birthday, the same spirit guide and his undying faith to stand by her side when he barely knew her. He was like a guardian angel, who would follow her anywhere without question just to make sure he kept an eye on her. It comforted her to know that there was something special about her and Dylan's bond.

All of these thoughts tumbled around in Mica's head, and she suddenly realized that Buddha had been walking her, not the other way around, and now they were at a building behind the temple on the hill. It was hidden from view. She hadn't seen it from the dorms and even walking to the temple you couldn't see it, but there it was. It was a large circular building with giant twenty-foot doors. The words read "Akashic Records" carved into a large stone above the double doors. Next to the door read, "No students allowed." Mica stood there, wondering what this building held and the doors opened. Mica backed up quickly and Ronak poked his head out.

"Hello, Mica." He smiled all knowingly.

Mica felt like she had been caught stealing. "Ronak! I wasn't going to go in, I just, well Buddha walked up here and I wasn't going to go in." Mica stuttered not wanting Ronak to think she disobeyed rules.

"Well, it just so happens that students aren't allowed in here, but since you haven't started classes yet, I think I can give you a tour." He smiled rebelliously, and Mica picked up Buddha, tucking him under her arm following Ronak inside before he changed his mind. She stopped in the doorway, craning her neck to see. It was a library. The secrecy of the building and the warning on the door made Mica think there might be magical instruments in here.

"Oh, a library. Cool," Mica exclaimed disappointed. Books towered from ground to ceiling in a perfectly circular room, a few green velvet chairs in the middle. There were two older men in indigo hoodies sitting in the chairs deep in thought. Ronak had a look of disappointment on his face.

"A library? Do you think I would sneak you into just any old library?" Ronak mentally summoned a book to the left about ten feet up on the shelf. It glided with ease towards Mica. She realized she needed to catch it and she set Buddha down and grabbed the book. The cover read:

Mica Moon 1/30/2038

(Domed World/ Frequency 648.99)

Life 8,304

Mica's eyes widened bigger than humanly possible.

Ronak smiled triumphantly, "Ahhh, so now you're interested? The Akashic Records is a record hall of all the words, thoughts and actions carried out by all humans in all worlds. It also contains a guide plan about your life from birth to death. Therefore, if you read it, you might influence your future. Try to open it."

Mica tried to lift open the cover and couldn't.

"That book knows whether or not you will heal the domed world." Ronak added. Now Mica really put some strength into it, pulling at the cover of the book with all her might, letting out a little grunt.

"Frustrating, isn't it?" Ronak smiled.

"Some things should not be known." He grabbed the book from her and opened it with ease, flipping through a few pages, before slamming it shut again, and sent it sailing back into the air to its place on the shelf.

"You can open it? What does it say?" Mica was desperate to know anything.

"Of course I can open it, I helped write it. I'm your spirit guide, Mica, I helped plan out your life before you were born."

"So, I'm just going to do everything in that book and I have no say?" Mica was frustrated.

"No, that book has a record of your current strengths, weaknesses, and actions to date and then also a plan for your highest potential. You have free will, so whether or not you live up to that potential is up to you."

"Do you think I can?" Mica asked.

"Of course, the Elders and I would never plan more for you than you can handle."

"Well, then if I can't open any books, why even come in here?"

"Because, this is also the hall of knowledge about actions and histories of all worlds within the universe. It is where we study and find solutions for current world problems. It's where we figured out how to save your world from the pollution, and contain the virus. It was only temporary of course. Now the domes are a curse and I'll be glad if you can free the people from them and heal that world."

"WHEN I free them not IF." Mica smiled.

"Ahhh, positive thinking, very nice. The Akashic Record Hall is also where highly evolved spirits like those two men over there, come to prepare knowledge for the Creator of other worlds."

"Creators, I've heard of them. Do they have the most important job?" Mica asked.

"There's only one Creator and it is the hardest job, but no more important than any other. All of the things you will do after you graduate will be important."

"If there is only one Creator, is he like....God?" Mica inquired.

Ronak let out a hearty laugh. "No, the Creator creates worlds FOR the Source, whom you call God in your world. All things come from Source. The Source is not a person, not male or female, it is simply the Source of all creation, the original conscious energy of unconditional love. We are all a piece of the Source."

"Oh," Mica said trying to grasp the concept.

"Well, I think that's enough for today. Did you receive your books and things?"

"Yes, thank you for all the clothes and stuff. One more question and then I'll go." Mica wanted to ask him about that word Namaste.

"You want to know what Namaste means?" Ronak said smiling.

"Yes! How did, oh never mind, yes what does it mean? They engraved it on my bed and said it again at the dinner last night."

Ronak bowed his head to Mica, teaching her one of the most important lessons in life.

"Namaste means, (I bow to you) in Sanskrit. To say Namaste to someone and bow your head means that you recognize the divine within them as well as within yourself. Mica, we are all one, we are all divine, everyone is equal and special. You say Namaste to a homeless person, a drug addict or a monk, there is no difference.

By recognizing the divine in someone, you are holding them in the light, helping them on their path for the best and highest good of the universe."

"Oh, ok, wow that's deep. I thought it might mean goodnight or something."

Ronak laughed.

"Just don't forget it's the highest form of respect you can show someone, to call someone your equal no matter who they are."

Mica bowed her head, "Namaste."

Ronak smiled, glad he had picked such a pure-hearted child.

"Namaste, Mica."

"One last thing I want to show you before I see you out." Ronak led Mica over to a table in the middle of the circular room, there was a large wooden rectangular studying table at least ten feet long. Laminated on the top of the table was a picture with about 500 people in all standing in front of the temple. On the bottom of the photograph it read, "Lightworkers for Humanity." Ronak pointed to a man. He was about 20 years old with brownish hair and wore a teal hoodie.

"Recognize him?"

Mica leaned in farther. He looked like her grandpa, only younger.

"Yes, it's your grandfather, he saved many worlds, and kept the domed world safe from darkness for a long time. I wanted to tell you that about two weeks ago he came to a meeting with the Elders just before he died and said the greatest gift he could give to the Universe was you, keeping you safe and leading you on your path. He said knowing he would die was no big deal, because he also knew you would live." Mica began to cry and turned her head away in embarrassment.

Ronak cradled her face by the chin and turned her towards him looking her straight in the eyes.

"Don't ever be ashamed of your tears, emotions are one of the most beautiful gifts we get to experience as human beings." Mica stood for a few moments staring into his wise eyes, she felt like she had known Ronak her whole life. Maybe she had and never knew. She looked at the picture for another moment, and afterward Ronak led her out of the building, he smiled at her.

"I agree with your grandfather, you are a great gift to the Universe. Enjoy tonight with your friends; we leave tomorrow morning at eight a.m." And with that he went back inside.

Mica walked with Buddha back down the spiral stone steps, feeling the culmination of her journey of the past few weeks. How long had it been? Eight or nine days? five years? It felt like forever. Tomorrow she would arrive back in the domed world, and the morning after that she would be called to act on everything she said she could do. She reached the dorms to see Dylan, Teensie and Luke sitting along the edge of the fountain.

"Hey, Buddha," Dylan called a greeting to Buddha as he trotted over to him, jumping up onto his lap and looked at Mica panting. Mica smiled, noticing Dylan and Buddha's bond.

"We leave tomorrow morning at 8 a.m," she told Dylan.

"Alright," he said, careful not to let her know he was nervous.

"Then tonight we celebrate!" Teensie screamed. "It's Saturday, school doesn't start until Monday, free time!" Teensie said all of this with her normal quirky energy that Mica had become dependent on for a change of scene.

"What did you have in mind?" Mica inquired.

"Party in the water tribe free spirit room, no Virgos allowed, of course. I'll spread the word!"

In seconds she was off like a car on a racetrack running towards a group of people.

Luke looked puzzled. "Did she say no Virgos? Why not, I'm a Virgo?"

Mica and Dylan smiled awkwardly.

"She's a bit whacky about certain astrological signs. Best to say you're an Aquarius or something else." Dylan offered.

"Okay, Weird."

"It's Saturday? That doesn't seem right?" Mica thought aloud.

"Time is different here than in other worlds." Luke said.

They sped through the rest of the day just relaxing and talking about school. When Mica and Dylan were alone she told him all about the Akashic Records. He was a bit jealous at first, but in the end excited that Mica had gotten to experience it. Before they knew it, the clock said seven and Mica and Dylan made there way to the free spirit room, where they had their orientation meeting the previous day. Above the door a handmade sign said, "Party." Mica and Dylan entered to find that the room was packed full of all kinds of students, some fire spirits wearing orange hoodies, and some Earth spirits wearing white hoodies. They scanned the crowd to find Teensie in the center of a circle, telling a story enthusiastically.

"Mica, Dylan over here." She waved them over.

"Why is it called the free spirit room?" Mica asked.

"Because you can do anything you want in here! You can be a free spirit, I'm thinking of holding a weekly prophecy card club here, no telepaths allowed of course. Have you seen Luke?" she asked affectionately.

"Um, no, we just got here."

"Oh, okay, I forgot that I haven't even asked his sign yet. I'll bet he's a Gemini. Has to be with bone structure like that."

"Bone structure" Dylan mouthed to Mica, trying to stifle a laugh.

They made their way around the room, introducing themselves, Mica was scanning auras and found that almost every person here really had a pure heart and good intentions. She was so used to the domed world where kids were spiteful and cruel. They met up with Luke and had an entertaining night with Teensie being a lively host. They met kids from a plethora of worlds with all kinds of gifts. It was all so fascinating and Mica couldn't wait to learn more. As the night wore on Dylan and Mica got tired and said their goodbyes walking back towards their rooms.

"I wonder how many worlds there are? Maybe if we screw up the domed world, it won't matter if there's so many more." Dylan thought aloud grinning sarcastically. Mica knew he wasn't serious.

"We'll be fine, don't you believe in me? You saw me heal that tree and Mark healed that water at Harvard. It's just like that on a MUCH bigger scale." Dylan smiled at her. Then Mica was reminded of her dream and her face darkened.

"What is it?" Dylan asked. Mica knew him to be an expert dream interpreter so she didn't mention anything. She feared that he would tell her it was a prophetic dream.

"Nothing, I'm fine." She smiled weakly. Dylan wasn't a specialist in girls, and he didn't need his crystal to tell him that when a girl said she was "fine" it usually meant the opposite. He didn't press her. The last thing she needed was stress.

Mica said goodnight and went up to her room. She was in the bathroom brushing her teeth when Teensie came in.

"Great party, right? Luke, is dreamy. I think we're definitely going to be the cool kids. We were the first ones to throw a party and your going to save an entire world. Since you're my suite mate that reflects onto me. Oh yea, we're soooo cool."

Mica spit toothpaste out laughing, "You're a trip Teensie, and I like it."

"Thanks. So, what happens if you don't heal that world?" Teensie asked more somber.

"Well the people are multiplying, but there's no room for growth and the resources for heat and food are slowly dwindling, AND the Nano technology used to make the domes is dying and would take years to figure out a stronger replacement. So, I imagine in the next few years life won't exist. The domes will fail and the virus will contaminate everyone and humans will wipe each other out in the process of trying to stay alive themselves. The blackness outside the domes will enter once the Nanobots collapse, which will slowly mutate and kill everyone if the virus doesn't. You know, world wars and all that horrid stuff."

For once, Teensie was speechless and Mica realized she had needed to vent that, to speak the truth about what really would happen without her. She needed the pressure now to help her succeed. "Oh, yeah that's bad. You want me to do a reading to tell you if you're going to be victorious?" Teensie said, quickly rebounding.

"A reading?"

"Jeez, what world are you from? Yeah, I spread out the prophecy cards for you and read them to tell you your future."

"Prophecy cards?" Mica was confused. The only thing they had like that in her world, were tarot cards.

"Prophesy cards help the non-natural telepaths to see the future." She flew out of the room and came back holding cards wrapped in purple silk.

"My mom hand-made them for me when I was six with her own original artwork. She's a Taurus." Teensie barged into Mica's room and plopped on her bed next to Buddha, who was sleeping.

"I like your room, it has good energy." Teensie smiled. She lay the purple silk on the bed and told Mica to sit across from her and shuffle the cards. Mica decided humoring Teensie wouldn't hurt so she mixed up the cards thinking of tomorrow. Teensie closed her eyes whispering something under her breath. Then she asked Mica to pick out four cards and lay them face down, which Mica did choosing carefully.

"Ahhh, I see." Teensie turned the card face up on the cloth. It was "the world" card, which had beautifully drawn colorful artwork, Mica wasn't expecting them to be so captivating. The card featured a blond-haired girl, who looked a lot like Mica, holding the world in the palms of her hands. Underneath in cursive it said, "The World."

"This card tells me that healing the domed world is your destiny. You will be greatly rewarded in life if you succeed." Teensie's usually comical voice was now deadpan and she wore a serious look.

She flipped over the next card. "Strength," Which showed a girl again eerily resembling Mica with a lion submissively in her arms next to her heart. "It will take every ounce of courage you have to do this, but you are strong enough to succeed."

She flipped the next card revealing the words "The Emperor." A boy with brown hair wore a golden crown, he smiled and brandished a sword.

"This card makes me think of Dylan and I see him helping you greatly; without him you would not be courageous, therefore you would not succeed."

"Okay, the last card is always the outcome card." Teensie flipped it over, her face dropping in a look of desperation. She immediately threw it back into the deck and smiled. "Oh, I've never been very good at this. I'm going to bed. Goodnight and good luck." She hugged Mica tightly then scooped up her purple cloth to leave. Mica grabbed her arm "What did that card say?"
Teensie looked down at her friend. "Do you really want to know?"

"No, I guess I don't, whatever it says. I am the master of my own destiny. Everything will be fine."

Teensie smiled at her friend and left, leaving Mica to her worst fears. Failure.

Mica lay awake for hours, replaying Teenise's look of shock and wondered what that card had said. Death, destruction, failure, doom? All of the possibilities swam around in Mica's head. She thought of Gran and of Nadia, Chloe and Dr. Culbertson, and hoped they were well. She knew by now the girls and boys from the Berkshire Preparatory orphanage would be in new homes and that helped her to rest easy for a bit. She thought of what Ronak had said about inviting Nadia, but that she would refuse and not leave Chloe. She thought that maybe since Nadia was so intuitive she would already know she had been invited.

Thinking of Nadia she drifted off to sleep, dreaming heavily again. This time she was by a creek in Sedona where she used to walk with Gran. It was one of the only natural running waters left in Arizona and although you couldn't touch it or drink it because it was contaminated, Mica still loved the sound of the running water. She stood there in her dream at an old spot she liked where a large dark tree overhung, blocking out the light. Nadia was crawling out of a tent; Mica heard rustling and Dylan walked out from behind the tree. Mica was aware that she was dreaming, which was an odd new feeling.

"How are you?" Nadia said.

"I'm dreaming," said Mica wondrously. Dylan just stood there listening.

Nadia smiled. "I know, I'm sending you and Dylan this dream to let you guys know that Chloe and my dad and I are all here in Sedona camping out waiting for your arrival. On our travels here we met thousands of supporters. Mica, it's really happening, people believe in you! But I also send this message in warning. Damian Black is here too, and he is putting as many of your followers as he can in jail. He also says he has proof of you and Dylan murdering World Leader Mullen and conspiring to blow up the domes tomorrow, not to save them. He has told anyone who sees you to turn you in or they will be incarcerated. Meet us by the creek and we will hide out until the healing. I miss you guys. See you soon."

And then Mica was flying upwards into a light filled room. She awoke at seven a.m. to her phone ringing.

"Hello," she said groggily.

"Did you get all that? In the dream from Nadia?" It was Dylan.

"Yeah, weird, is that what's it's like for you all the time?" she asked.

"Pretty much."

"Wow, you must not sleep very much," she observed. "Lets meet in an hour at the fountain."

Mica hung up and went to Buddha's doghouse. She stuck her head inside and he looked up.

"Boo, I'm going on a trip and I'm going to leave you here." He cocked his head to the side flipping his ear over. "I want you to be safe and I need something to come back to." Mica kissed the top of his furry head and left a note in the bathroom for Teensie to feed and walk him. She didn't know how long she would be gone; there was a horrid chance she might never come back. She packed the Shiva Lingham and some clothes in a bag and set out to meet Dylan. With that she came one step closer to her destiny.

Chapter Eleven
The Domed World

Ronak was waiting for them by the fountain. He stood in jeans and an indigo long-sleeved t-shirt with a small woman with red curly hair. Mica knew at once this was Teensie's mother, the likeness was unmistakable. She too stood against the fountain in jeans and a silver colored t-shirt. Ronak spoke, "This is Cyndi Love, and she will be our traveler today."

"So Teensie's full name is Teensie Love?" Mica said giggling.

"So it's obvious I'm her mother? Her name is adorable isn't it?" Cyndi asked with the same quirky persona as Teensie.

"Oh, yes it is," Mica replied, not wanting her to think she was making fun of her daughter.

"Mica why don't you get acquainted with Cyndi while I talk to Dylan." Ronak took Dylan over to a large weeping willow until they were out of earshot.

"Dylan, I fear giving you a weapon that could hurt another human being or yourself, but I cannot let you go into this task unarmed. This is your last chance to back out. I could escort Mica to make sure she's safe and you can stay here." Ronak held a knife in his hand, it sat on top of a leather sheath with a golden circle symbol carved into the leather. The blade was about 6 inches long and glimmered emerald green.

Dylan looked Ronak in the eyes. He felt that this man knew without Dylan saying a word why he must go.

"You know I must go." Dylan said.

"Dylan, do you know what your gift is? Why you are here?"

Dylan was caught off-guard by the question. "Yeah, I'm a telepath and prophetic dreamer." Dylan said, now a little unsure if that was true.

"No, you're not." Ronak said plainly. "Your moldavite crystal gives you the messages and dreams. Without it, you wouldn't be telepathic."

Dylan felt a pang of uncertainty, followed by anger. Why was Ronak saying all of this? "Then why even invite me here, if I have no gift?" Dylan said angrily.

Ronak was patient. "I didn't say you had NO gift, I said mental telepathy wasn't it. Every fifty years the Universe sends us a Creator. A being that can structure entire continents and worlds with his mind, his energy and his intent. Every fifty years this person comes here and trains with the old Creator to keep the circle of life going. Dylan, YOU are the Creator, and if you go with Mica and do not return, all future worlds will cease to exist. The current Creator will die before a new one has been trained and the cycle will break.

I don't think Damian Black knows you're the Creator, but if he does he will stop at nothing to have you, with his mind control abilities he could make you create other worlds for him, dark worlds.

He must never find out that you are the Creator. You're safe here, but I cannot guarantee your safety outside of this world.

This knife was forged with melted bits of moldavite crystal. It's a killing knife Dylan, created to keep you safe. When thrust into someone and left long enough inside their skin, it begins to suck out their aura. You could stab someone in the foot, but if left in their skin for more than a few minutes they would die as if you struck them in the heart. We do not promote violence at this school but this weapon is crucial for the existence of the Universe because the darkness will always try to capture or harm the Creator. It's a life of much danger. You have no need for this weapon inside this school. You have free will, so I'm going to ask you one more time, must you go with her?"

Dylan froze. For once he wasn't sure whether or not to go. The Creator? Could that be? Mica was the special one, not him. The crystal in his ear whispered softly. *"You are the Creator but she can't do it without you. Follow your heart."* Dylan thought of Mica going without him and not succeeding. It would crush her and he couldn't let all of those people die. Dylan swallowed hard "I'm going and will come back alive!" He grabbed the knife and as his skin touched the handle the crystal in his braid radiated green light as did the long 6 inch blade. Dylan slid it into the leather sheath and then the back waistband of his pants.

They set off back to the fountain, Mica and Cyndi were laughing as they approached.

"Ready?" Cyndi asked.

"Yes," Ronak said trying not to show emotion. He knew Mica could detect the slightest bit of fear in his aura and so he remained calm. "As you are aware, we need to go to Sedona, Arizona in the domed world."

"Wait, why do we need a traveler? Can't you go in and out of other worlds, Ronak?" Dylan inquired.

"Yes, I can go wherever I want whenever I want, but to transport you two we need a professional traveler to hold all of us in their minds otherwise I might lose you in some random dimension. And since we're fast-forwarding in time and space, it's best to leave it to the professionals so we arrive in one piece. Cyndi is a natural, she traveled for the first time at two years old."

"Scared the crap out of my parents!" Cyndi interjected happily.

"Oh, OK," Dylan gulped, not wanting to be lost in a random dimension without all of his pieces. He touched the knife through his shirt wondering when he should tell Mica he was the Creator. He decided it was best to wait until after the healing, he didn't even know what being the Creator meant.

"You will learn in my class to do basic world traveling of yourself but not until your green year. Even then you will need to call on a traveler to move large groups or go forward in time or space. Okay then, hold hands." Cyndi instructed.

They all stood in a circle and when Mica joined hands with Cyndi and Dylan, she felt a pulling that was unlike traveling with the Shiva Lingham, it was more graceful, more thought out. They landed on their feet comfortably and Mica heard the faint sound of a running creek. As she regained her sense of location, she saw her favorite tree and the tent from her dream. Nadia poked her head out, smiling. Mica looked at Ronak. "How did you know we needed to come here?"

Ronak merely smiled.

"Well, I've got more assignments today," Cyndi said. "Ronak, you can get back on your own. Good luck kids, see you Monday in class," Cyndi added in a cheery voice. She closed her eyes, and a second later vanished from sight.

Nadia, her father and Chloe walked over. They all embraced and Ronak asked to speak to Nadia and her father alone. As they walked away Chloe looked hurt.

"Why would he want to talk to her alone?" Chloe asked.

Mica knew why. "Well, when we left your dad's house in Boston, we arrived in a world that's a school for children with gifts like Nadia's and so I think he's inviting her, but don't worry, I'm sure she won't leave you."

"Oh," was all Chloe said.

Dylan changed the subject, "So, how long have you guys been in Sedona?"

Chloe perked up. "Well, it's a fascinating story. We were in Boston and Nadia started getting visions that you guys would be here so we made our way down the country, jumping from train to train, taking electric cars and riding bikes. Along the way, people helped us because we were on the Harvard news tape that Mark Densy made, and they knew we were your supporters. There are underground safe houses all across the country and the password is Freeworld." Chloe smiled and the continued. "We made it here about three days ago, and even though Nadia knows your grandma lives here, we haven't gone to her because Dad said it would get her in trouble." Mica felt a sting in her throat, she had totally forgotten about Gran in all the excitement of school, now she missed her terribly and wanted to see her.

Dylan picked up on her thoughts. "Her house is being watched, I guarantee it. Just wait and we can see her tomorrow after everything works out." He smiled as Ronak made his way back with Nadia and Dr. Culbertson, who all wore unreadable poker faces.

Ronak walked up to Mica. "This is where I leave you. If you need me, just call and I will show up, but I cannot stay and interfere. This is your destiny and you must do it alone, without my help." Mica breathed deeply, she was afraid of that. "And you can do it," he added with a smile. He grabbed her shoulders and squeezed. He turned to Dylan and spoke into his mind without moving his lips. *Take care of her, stay near the water where you can use the Shiva Lingham to escape if things go badly, and only use the knife if your life is in danger.* Dylan nodded slightly.

"Goodbye kids." Ronak said. It was the hardest part of being a spirit guide. Having to leave and let your students make mistakes or do things without you, but being a guide was merely that. You could guide them, not do everything for them. What would they learn? How would they grow if you did that? So Ronak left his two subjects and watched them from a far. He kept his mind tuned to Mica and Dylan at all times and would for the rest of their lives. They had forged a bond with Ronak that could never be broken. As a spirit guide that was what made you feel whole, that bond, that link.

Nadia felt the uneasiness of her sister and spoke out loud. "I'm not going," she said simply.

Chloe smiled, but then looked sullen. "Well, maybe you should, I mean if you're needed." Chloe said. Nadia wasn't just her sister or best friend, she was her twin! A complete carbon copy of her and although they were different people, Chloe felt that Nadia was the only one on Earth who knew how she felt at all times.

"I'm not going and that's that," Nadia exclaimed. Chloe smiled loving her sister for that matter-o-fact answer. Her dad however looked disappointed.

"Well, Mica and Dylan we are so glad to have met up with you again, funny how the world works, bringing us back together. Or funny how my daughter works I should say." He looked at Nadia and they all laughed.

"Less than twenty-four hours from now we will be walking out of the domes as free people!" he said. The thought hadn't occurred to Mica until now. How was she actually going to remove the domes? She knew she could heal the plants and water and people but hadn't really thought about the actual plastic-like structures that dot the entire world. Everyone everywhere was expecting to be free. Nadia spoke into her mind, saying "*It will work itself out,*" and smiled.

"I'm going to scope the area and make sure we're alone and then we can get the electric grill going and have some breakfast. Dylan would you help me?" Dr. Culbertson asked.

"Yeah," Dylan said, he was spacing out thinking about being the Creator, Ronak must be mistaken he had never created anything in his life. As Dylan and Dr. Culbertson walked off he spoke to Dylan in confidence.

"Having two daughters is amazing, don't get me wrong, but sometimes you just need another man around, I'm glad for your company. Chloe has been screaming at every bug in sight and we had to beg her to even camp here." Dylan laughed at the thought of Chloe being attacked by moths but figured it must be hard being a single dad and raising two girls.

"Well, maybe we can play football or something one of these days." Dylan replied.

"I love football! I was the king of the pigskin in college."

"Oh, yeah, you're American. I actually meant soccer. Sorry." Dylan was embarrassed he had gotten him all excited. "But maybe you could teach me American football?" Dylan added, hoping to redeem himself.

"Or you could teach me soccer?" They smiled and Dylan felt a little piece of him cry out as he thought of what he had been missing in his life because he didn't have parents. Just walking along this creek and talking about random things is a memory Dylan would cherish. They scouted the creek in every direction, making sure they were alone.

After they set up the grill and ate eggs and sausage, Mica and Dylan told stories of The Universal School of Lightworkers. Everyone laughed when Mica described Teensie and her weird Virgo phobia and bubbling personality. When Mica told them about her school schedule and the classes they would take, Dr. Culbertson perked up. He said he wished he was a kid with gifts and that he could have gone to this school. He asked about maybe getting a day pass just to see someone levitate and defy the laws of gravity. In turn the twins told Mica and Dylan about the people they'd met on their travels.

Though Chloe was letting Nadia speak more now, she often interjected finishing her sentences. Nadia began telling Mica about all of the people in Los Angeles who had put up twenty-foot signs saying "Support Mica, Freeworld!" and how the government took them down. Then Chloe would interject, telling them that they would then spray paint things like "August 15th, Freeworld," on another building. Some rogue TV stations had replayed the newscast tape of Mark twenty-fours hours straight until Black had shut them down. People were gathering in groups, ready for the day of the healing but Black forced people into hiding, threatening to put them in jail for supporting Mica and her supposed treason.

Dr. Culbertson looked distressed. "Now, Mica, I know this might upset you but Black is saying that you're not really going to heal the Earth tomorrow at sunrise, he says he has intelligence that you're going to blow up the domes. That unless people turn you in, we will all die. He says you're a terrorist masked as a young innocent child, but working for a bad group of radicals. There are large enough numbers of people who believe him, so you must stay here at the tent out of sight. You can be anywhere when you heal as long as it's outside, right?"

Mica nodded, feeling anger toward Damian Black. "I guess I shouldn't have come back here to Sedona because I'm from here, and they will be looking for me, but my healing energy was discovered here and I just feel like I'm most powerful in this place."

"Well, I think we're pretty well hidden and if we have to fight we can. I have an old family heirloom that I think still works. It's from 2007." Dr. Culbertson said and pulled out a sleek black gun and everyone whistled in amazement. "It's a Glock Nine. My father was a cop in New York City and I'll use it if I have too. I know it's a bit ancient and outlawed, but it worked fine in those days." He had a wild look about him, like he had been waiting his whole life to shoot that gun off.

"Well, we shouldn't really harm other people. In those days they had hundreds of deaths a year from guns." Mica said.

Dylan sat up straighter. "Well, we will do what it takes. If they're trying to hurt us, are we supposed to be killed so we can die with good karma?" Dylan wasn't trying to be mean, but sometimes Mica was too naive.

"I guess not." Mica looked down, not really wanting to argue about it and cringed at the thought of killing someone or being killed.

As the afternoon rolled on, Mica grew antsy. She walked along the creek only going about hundred feet from the tent and found Dylan peeking from behind a tree watching her. She wanted to be alone. She felt like she should be preparing or doing something. She sat on a rock near the creek, crossing her legs and closing her eyes. She centered in on her breathing, slowing down her heart rate. She admitted to herself that she was nervous and focused on the sound of the creek, the rustling leaves and the cold stone beneath her. She opened her eyes halfway and saw the golden light emanating from her aura and bathing the surrounding trees, and red rock Earth. She pulled the energy back. Just testing.

She collected her thoughts and walked back to the others. They all had dinner by the grill, but the meal was different than any of the others they'd shared that day. The collective tone was somber, everyone in the group was feeling the pressure. Mica could barely take the silence, the weight of her task. If she failed to heal the Earth she'd use the Shiva Lingham and go to a world where no one knew her, she wouldn't return back to the school to be ridiculed.

But she knew she wouldn't do that, life was about accepting that rejection can happen and taking a chance. At last, tired of the wheels spinning in her mind, she looked at Nadia's dad and asked him to tell them a story.

He smiled warmly, a fatherly smile. "Well, when the girls were turning six, their mother and I, still together then, went shopping for their birthday presents. We wrapped and hid them in the closet. We had gotten them each the same thing, a doll set complete with playhouse and hairbrushes. Later that night at dinner, Nadia blurted out, 'We don't want dolls! I want an art set and Chloe wants a tree house,' " They all laughed.

"I remember that!" Exclaimed Nadia.

"Me too," Chloe said, giggling.

Dr. Culbertson laughed and carried on.

"Her mother and I were shocked, for a second, and then their mother started yelling furiously at Nadia for opening the gifts early, but I went to the closet to check. As you can guess they were still wrapped and that was the beginning of my knowledge of Nadia's gift and the end of my marriage to their mother." He looked at the grill transfixed by the glowing coils.

"She never believed in me," Nadia said robotically.

"And I never got my tree house," Chloe said, breaking the silence. They all smiled and traded childhood stories for the next two hours. Mica told stories about her and Gran. Dylan told them of ancient gypsy traditions, which made Mica recall that her own dad had been a gypsy, an English gypsy. Mica absent-mindedly felt inside her shirt to rub the rose quartz heart. A calming, loving feeling washed over her and she soaked it up. After they had their fill of conversation, the girls went in the tent to sleep and the boys lay out in front in sleeping bags.

Dr. Culbertson spoke to Dylan once the girls were out of earshot. "I think it's wise if one of us stays awake and watches for trouble. I'll take the first watch and wake you in a couple of hours."

"Good idea," Dylan said, lying in his sleeping bag, pulling out the knife from his pants waistband and placing it under his rolled up sweater, which served as a makeshift pillow. As Dylan slept, he dreamt of a stage like the one at a rock concert, but people didn't look happy. As he looked closer, he realized there was no band, just two empty nooses that hung in the air with two empty chairs right below them. Fear gripped him and he woke up. His crystal shook the braid in his hair but wasn't saying anything. It was like someone was blocking its message.

Dr. Culbertson noticed him awaking. "Everything okay?"
Finally two weak words sifted from the crystal into his ear. *Imminent danger*.

"They're here," Dylan spoke the words with absolute certainty. Then he heard a ripping sound behind him as the tent was sliced open from behind. Someone must have come up the creek and made their way up to the camp from behind. Dylan sprang into action, tucking the knife into his waistband and running at the tent full speed, ready to use the knife when needed. But they were outmanned. Twenty men in black government uniforms held all three girls, duct tape already around their mouths. Dylan barely made out rope hanging from the trees and realized they had entered from above, pouncing on the tent like tigers.

In one swift movement, three men grabbed Dylan and Dr. Culbertson, and then Damian Black emerged from behind a tree. He poked into Mica's tent, grabbing the purple bag and making sure the Shiva Lingham was inside.

"Well done. Back to the jailhouse, they hang in the morning. At sunrise exactly." A smile flickered on Black's lips like that of a reptile. Dylan realized his dream was a premonition; they would hang in front of the town. Dylan searched his brain for any remnants of memory from the dream that would help him. He hadn't actually seen them hanging in the nooses, they'd been empty, so hopefully that meant their futures were still to be decided.

"You're a coward," Dylan spat. "You're afraid of Mica succeeding. You know she can do it."

Black glided over to Dylan as if he were floating. "You're an idiot for helping her on this pursuit and I shall deal with you personally. Tape their filthy mouths shut!"

The men taped Dylan and Dr. Culbertson's mouths and led them up the hill away from the creek. They were loaded into a large SUV and headed north towards town. In the car, Damian sat in front in the passenger seat, while the others were in the back. As they came up to the Highway 89, Nadia's voice echoed in Mica's head. She could see Nadia's aura reaching out to her through the silver chord, and another chord was going to Damian Black. *"Black is trying to read your thoughts, I'm holding him off, but you must take your energy down a notch, make your aura very small and close your mind, imagine a giant steel dome over your head. Do it now!"* Mica looked at her body, her aura was agitated, a reddish orange and it glowed about three feet off her body.

She closed her eyes and imagined her inner light shrinking. She pulled her aura in close to her body and imagined a metal salad bowl over her head. Black whipped around and looked right at Mica. "Ahhh, they are teaching you well at that school. Do they still claim that you will be doing good for humanity? Or are they telling the truth now, that you will be stripped of your freedom and be called upon to live a penniless life with no fame or fortune." He spun around and ripped the tape off of Mica's mouth, but she didn't give him the satisfaction of crying out from the sting.

"Those with pure hearts have no need for fame or fortune!" Mica said breathlessly.

"Pure hearts! Oh you sound like one of the Elders themselves. I left that school and started using my power for all it could be and look at me now, I'm the World Leader, the way I should have been long ago. Instead they gave it to your grandfather. Well, look at him now." He shoved the tape back over Mica's mouth as she started screaming a retort.

A phone chirped in the front seat. Damian Black answered.

"This is World Leader Black." Then he paused. "Lovely, tell the news stations to run the story. I have caught the terrorists and they will hang in a public execution to show my people a lesson. Follow me and you are safe, but try and terrorize and make falsehoods at my people and you will pay. Tomorrow at sunrise, Mica and Dylan will hang. So much for their plan to blow up the domes."

He slammed the phone shut as they pulled into the sheriff's office. Mica and Dylan were placed in separate cells, as were Nadia, Chloe, and their father. Black told the guards to keep their mouths taped so there was no chance they could communicate.

The cells were encircled by bars, so Mica could see Dylan a few feet away and Nadia pressed against the bars next to the cell that her father was in.

Black and a big guard came into Mica's cell, dangling some sort of contraption. Dylan stood up, helpless if they were going to hurt her. The guard walked over and placed Mica's hands behind her back into something that looked like handcuffs with hollow leather balls at the ends. He forced Mica's hands into fists and placed them in each leather ball, locking the metal wrist cuff together. Black smirked and looked at the guard.

"From now until her death if those are taken off, you will die." He grabbed Mica's hair.

"You won't be healing anything! You can tell your grandfather I said hello when you see him. Oh, and if you try and pull a stunt like the one at Harvard, taking energy from any of my guards' hearts, I'll kill Dylan right in front of you." He let go of her hair, shoving her back. Dylan's heart broke as he saw a tear running down her dirty cheek. Black and the guard locked the cell behind them and left.

Dylan had never tried to speak telepathically, but he knew he could talk to his crystal so he tried something.

"Crystal, tell Nadia to tell Mica everything's going to be okay, tell her we can still do this, I believe in her, more than ever."

Dylan was desperate to save Mica from her heartache; he could feel her pain from across the room. A few seconds later, Dylan knew Nadia had received and delivered the message, because Mica looked right at him and smiled with her eyes, looking more beautiful than he had ever seen. The duct tape on her mouth bunched and he knew she was glad for his sentiments, because she was smiling.

Mica walked over to the small plastic covered mattress and lay down, curling into a ball. She missed her parents. It was one thing to grow up without ever having met them so you didn't really miss them, and another to see them for a brief while as spirits and then have them ripped away, like dangling candy in front of a child. She missed Gran and Buddha and Teensie. She wondered if her grandpa was watching her and if he was disappointed. She longed to be back at school in the water spirit dorms with all of the children who were just like her. She thought that the Elders were cruel to have aloud her to get into this miserable mess. Why couldn't they just send another more qualified healer to do this? She was only fourteen.

Now she had gotten all of her friends into this mess too and she had no Shiva Lingham and Damian Black had no aura for her to use to defend herself. She was at the mercy of fate. Even though she was uneasy, exhaustion took over. It was after 3 a.m. when Mica fell asleep, a dreamless void in which her body called out to the universe pleading not to be snuffed out like the flame of a candle by the wrath of Damian Black.

Chapter Twelve
The Hanging

Mica awoke groggily to footsteps. Each click on the concrete twisted her nerves into a tightrope. She looked up and saw four men coming down the hall. One was unmistakably Damian Black, his lanky body and superior strut were characteristics Mica would never forget. He paused at Dylan's cell.

"I'll take you first, Dylan, as I did promise you special treatment. Mica, you can follow us and have a front row seat to watch your beloved friend perish forever. Then the entire town can observe the famous healer hang for treason. I'll be the savior, and your friends can be evacuated by HAZMAT to take a nice trip outside the domes." He said with a sick joy in his voice.

He opened the door and grabbed Dylan by the back of his neck; Mica stood powerless. It must have been around 5 a.m., because when Dylan went outside, it was still dark, just the beginning of a faint glow. This coward Damian Black wanted to watch Mica stand helplessly on that stage during the time when she promised to heal the world and then kill her for no reason. Dylan detested Damian Black and wondered how it had all come down to this. After everything they had been through, Dylan truly believed that it could be done, and now Mica wasn't being given the chance. Dylan wasn't afraid to die, not afraid of what awaited him on the other side, not even afraid that there was no other side, just that he was letting the world down, the Universe, Ronak, Mica, everyone. As Dylan walked to his impending death, he admitted to himself that he felt for Mica in a way that he had never felt before.

As they rounded the corner, Dylan's walk stiffened and he almost stumbled. Over 2,000 people, in lifeless poses like wilted flowers, faced a large wooden makeshift stage, two nooses hung over the stage and it reminded him of the Salem witch trials. Dylan's dream was coming true, as they all had.

Black slipped the noose around Dylan's neck, ripping off the duct tape, and stood him on a chair. A guard, a foot away, seemed ready to pounce at the slightest move.

Black screamed to the crowd, "This boy has threatened our very existence. If I hadn't caught him and the girl, and stopped them and their elaborate plans to blow up the domes, you would have all been dead in a few minutes. As new World Leader, I send out a message to all of those who terrorize the human race. Unlike the late World Leader, I do not preach about peace and yet do nothing to stop violence, look where that got you. Terrorists have been making plans for years to kill us off and Mullen never knew. He was too high on his peace cloud. So I'm going to stop this betrayal right here and now."

............................★★★............................

A few moments after Black took Dylan, four guards came to get Mica. She refused to meet the faces of these low men. Nadia wanted to communicate telepathically, to say something, anything to her dear friend, but couldn't find the words. Psychically, every time Nadia asked to see the future of the healing she saw a closed door, which meant she was not allowed to see the outcome, and so she could not give false words of encouragement to her dear friend. All she could offer was the truth.

Nadia spoke to Mica's mind in one final attempt to bring the poor girl peace. *"We will never forget you, you have changed my life forever."* Mica looked like an angel walking to get her wings clipped. Mica looked at Nadia and tried to convey the love she had for her through her eyes.

They marched Mica out into the early morning darkness. Then they reached the illuminated stage, where lights shone on it like a ballpark field. What Mica saw made her cry, possibly her last tears on Earth. Thousands of people stood in front of the stage where Dylan stood on a chair with a noose around his neck. People's faces were downcast, as if they had come to support Mica, not Damian Black, but they couldn't show it for fear of death themselves. Black's speech concluded when the sun peeked out from the reddish mountains.

Then the air changed just a bit and Mica felt electricity flowing onto her face.

The moment of her life was now and people around the world were going to place their hands on the ground sending their love. Mica knew that people counted on her to at least try. Here she was handcuffed with four grown men holding her up and Black was on the stage and Dylan was in a noose ready to die for her. Then her heart threatened to stop beating at the shock and awe of all 2,000 people dropping to their knees.

Black wailed, "Bring her to me NOW!!!"

Then Mica heard an unmistakable click and her handcuffs fell to the ground with a poetic clink and the four guards kneeled and placed their hands on the cool red Earth. One of them looked up and said, "We believe in you."

Black was enraged by this and kicked the chair that held up Dylan. Dylan reached up to pull the rope away from his neck, fighting for breath. Mica screamed. But then she felt the familiar hands at her back, and she had to decide whether to save Dylan or the world. Dylan kept pulling at the rope to breathe, in one final attempt, with his last breath, he hoarsely screamed, "Mica, KNEEL!"

As Mica dropped she had tears in her eyes, and then she pleaded with mother Earth, "Thank you for giving us shelter, water, grain, sun and comfort. Heal please, we love you, we need you to be restored. Heal the people, cure the virus." As her hands reached the dirt, she could feel each grain of sand crying out in thanks, the entire ground for as far as Mica could see was glowing.

She looked up at the 2,000 kneeling people and they were covered in a caramel glow of healing energy. Mica concentrated and pushed with all her might, emitting the largest amount of healing light into the Earth that she had ever summoned in her life. Her hands were met by a sonic boom of light, blasting her off her feet and into the air, knocking her out cold on the hard ground.

Just as Mica was about to kneel, Dylan's crystal whispered *knife* in his ear. He had forgotten all about it and Black had never taken it away. He was seeing black dots and knew he only had moments before he'd pass out. He reached behind himself and cut the rope free in seconds. He lay there on the stage, his vision returning and catching his breath. He jumped up and saw that Black was halfway to Mica when her hands hit the ground, and then moments later she flew backwards and Dylan was running.

Mica awoke an instant later to the ground rumbling like a stomach that hadn't eaten in years. A huge crack threatened to engulf her as Black screamed, "Noooooo." The Earth was shaking and rattling, cracking noises were sounding all around, but they were met with cheers from the distant crowd. Mother Earth was unwrapping herself and shedding her un-pure skin. Black reached Mica and slipped his hands around her throat but Dylan was on him in seconds, driving the knife into his back. But then in a deadly counter movement, Black let go of Mica and pulled the knife out of his back barely flinching and like a maniac drove it into Dylan's chest.

"NOOOO! Ronak Help! Help! Help!" Mica screamed. Black stumbled backward and flinched at the mention of Ronak's name.

"Ronaaak!" Mica wailed.

Ronak heard Mica's call and knew by the urgency he had only seconds to act. He mentally summoned Cyndi, Teensie's mom to no avail. He could teleport to Mica's side but needed a traveler to bring Mica and Dylan back and they couldn't use the Shiva Lingham or they wouldn't be calling. He arrived outside Teensie's door in seconds, she answered sleepily.

"Teensie, Mica and Dylan are in trouble, and I need a traveler to bring them back here, can you do it?"

Teensie closed her eyes and Ronak heard Mica call again loudly inside his head. Teensie carefully separated the planets and universes until she saw the domed world clearly, then she saw Mica's energy at once, but failed to find Dylan.

"I can get us to Mica, but I can't find Dylan." She held out her hand.

"We might be too late," Ronak said, grabbing her small fingers and feeling the pull. They arrived in Sedona on the red rocky soil in no time and Ronak's fears were well founded.

Dylan lay motionless with the knife in his chest, bleeding freely, while Black, a few feet away, was choking the life out of Mica, her skin turning blue. The ground shook and people in the distance were cheering and running. Mica had forgotten about her mother's rose quartz heart necklace. She thought of it now because it burned hot on her skin, but not nearly as hot as it was to Damian Black. It singed the skin off his hands; Mica could smell his burning flesh, with what little breath she had left. For a moment, he let go to look at his hands and Mica took that second to draw in a much-needed gulp of air. Ronak levitated onto Black's back, instantly ripping him away from her.

"Hello old friend," Ronak said, smiling mockingly and dropping Black from ten feet in the air.

"Teensie, get them back to the temple, NOW!" Ronak bellowed.

Teensie grabbed Dylan's cold hand and Mica made a run towards them, but Black tried to grab her and Ronak intervened again, grabbing Black by the throat and levitating them both high up in the air. As Mica ran towards Dylan, her soul split in two. Dylan had no aura, he was dead... She held his lifeless hand feeling no familiar shock, as Teensie held the other.

They arrived inside the temple, all holding onto Dylan's lifeless body and Mica hovered over him crying. Teensie stumbled backwards in shock. Then out of nowhere, all twelve Elders materialized in a circle around Dylan. They held out their hands, some held crystal wands with precise beams of energy shooting out of them. They levitated Dylan's body into the air, slowly pulling the knife out of his chest and floating it to the ground a few feet away. Mica let him float up easily, suspended in mid-air.

"Please help, he's all I have, he saved my life!" Desperation didn't even describe what she was feeling. She prayed he would be whole again, because a part of her felt dead as well.

A male Elder spoke, "Mica you are the greatest healer we have ever known to exist in one human body. You can save him, we will help. I put a bubble of protection around him before he left, and I will release it now. He will have a faint ball of life force energy left. But you must give him the breath of life, and breathe your divine essence into his mouth, restoring his beautiful soul or his inner light will expire."

Mica would do anything. As the Elder removed the bubble that contained Dylan's aura, a dark gold glow the size of a dime flickered in the middle of his chest. All of the Elders were feeding Dylan energy, but the little ball in his chest was sucking it so fast and not growing any bigger.

Mica walked closer to Dylan's floating body and grabbed his face and opened his lips. "Dylan, it's all my fault. I can't live without you, please come back to me." She was weeping in silence. She put her lips over his and felt that electric spark and breathed her essence into him. She took her hands and put it over his heart, gently rubbing and flooding it with green healing light. Silence. And then boom... boom... boom.... His heart began beating and with each beat, his body began sucking up the Elders' energy and distributing it throughout his limbs. The energy looked like glowing blood flowing through each vein and encompassing his flesh.

Mica went over to his mouth again and breathed into it, willing her life force to merge with his. "Breathe," she whispered. Dylan lay still, then he gasped for air, startling Mica and bringing her to her knees.

"Thank you, thank you, thank you." She wept. The Elders slowly lowered him and started humming a beautiful chant. Then a woman came in, Reva, wearing peach robes with a burning bundle of leaves and she fanned them around the room.

Dylan still lay with his eyes closed, appearing unconscious, but his heart beat and he was breathing. Mica sat up and placed her hands over him, flooding him with light. She was so tired. She'd used so much energy to heal the domed world, which just then, for a moment she didn't even care about. She would sit here and give and give until Dylan woke up. That's all she wanted. The Elders chanted and hummed for the next few hours as Mica silently healed Dylan, the room a ball of light. Teensie had gone in search of her mom, and Ronak had popped in to say Black had escaped to another world. Then he'd popped back out.

After another hour, Dylan abruptly awoke panting, glancing around wildly. Seeing Mica, he grabbed her and pulled her close, holding her for a few minutes. His breathing was ragged and panicky but holding Mica close he began to match his breath intake to hers, breathing as one. He smelled her hair, touched her face, couldn't believe she was here, that he was here. Mica couldn't speak; she was relieved and shocked; he'd been raised from the dead. Dylan pulled back and lifted up his shirt, to reveal a faint scar over his heart where the knife had been. But it was healed, completely healed.

All of the Elders put down their hands and the woman in an indigo hoodie spoke, "Dylan, we are so pleased that you have decided to come back to Earth and help your fellow humans. Mica saved your life, without you she cannot live in purpose, you are blessed to have the worship of such a special angel and we are blessed for your existence. Because without you, the Universe would not evolve."

Dylan couldn't find his voice. After a moment of silence, the woman in the peach robes had re-entered the room, rolling in a giant hollow glass ball on a stand with wheels. She approached a male Elder setting it in front of him. The Elder motioned to the ball.

"This, Mica and Dylan, is a Universe Sphere. You can see anything that is going on at any time in any part of the Universe. Come closer." Dylan leaned on Mica for support as they moved closer and they noticed pictures projected onto the sphere like a movie screen.

Mica and Dylan stood there, staring at all of the people running out of the domes in California and swimming in the ocean! The air was clear, the water was crystal blue, and the sky was blazing! Mica couldn't believe the real sky was so beautiful and the sun was so huge but not burning people. The screen flashed fast, showing Gran smiling and crying, hugging her neighbor. It flashed to the little boy outside the domes, with his arms in the air spinning around. He looked so healthy and hundreds of people were behind him running. Then it flashed to Chloe, Nadia and their dad. Everyone was fine. Then the screen showed India. Everyone was running to the river and bowing on their knees, putting their arms up in the air, giving thanks. It was a miracle, Mica thought.

"As you can see, your friends are safe. The domed world has been healed, the contaminated have been healed and the virus is destroyed. The Earthquake has ripped huge cracks in the domed structures and they are slowly breaking down. People are running out, people are free. The people that were trapped on the outside are healthy and all is well, you have succeeded, Mica," the Elder woman said rolling the ball back to Reva.

Mica and Dylan smiled grabbing hands. They had done it, they had saved the world.

Dylan wanted so badly to tell her of his experience, that he WAS the Creator but it wasn't the right time. He kept staring at her, wondering if he was really back, if she was real.

Ronak appeared in the air just inside the temple, carrying the purple bag holding the Shiva Lingham and handed it to Mica. Mica ran to him and hugged him, not letting go for the longest time, and squeezing hard.

"You're the best guide ever! I love you. Thank you. Don't ever leave us!"

"I won't, I mean I can't, but if I could, I wouldn't." He smiled.

Ronak walked up to Dylan. "Sorry about giving you the knife, but I knew you would need it even if it did hurt you."

Dylan smiled. "Without it I would have been dead, But with it I was dead too, so...," they all laughed.

Dylan patted Ronak's back, "Thank you."

Dylan and Mica thanked all of the Elders and then Ronak brought them underground, below the pyramid building, into what he said was the crystal-healing chamber. A row of twenty tubes lined a long room with dim lights. The crystal tubes were clear, carved perfectly from large precious stones and stuffed with fluffy bedding for healing and comfort. Mica was so tired, and yet she mumbled questions at Ronak.

"How are Buddha and Gran? Is the domed world really all better?"

"Yes, Mica you saw it, you're going to need to rest now. You have given energy to save an entire world, and not to mention Dylan, so I think you deserve some sleep. Teensie is taking care of Buddha, Gran is fine, and the people are moving out of the domes cheering your name in the streets, reclaiming nature with respect."

Mica crawled into the crystal tube and fell fast asleep. Dylan, right beside her, did the same. Mica was regenerating her healing energy, and Dylan regenerated his entire existence. Ronak knew they would need this extra healing before going back out into the school and starting classes. The crystal chambers glowed with energy as they slept.

Ronak stood for awhile, just watching his two young students. If only they knew, this was just the beginning of a very complicated life with much danger. They were more extraordinary than they could possibly realize. The Universe needed them as they needed it. Together their souls could accomplish anything.